A Candlelight Ecstasy Romance™

IT WAS A SURE ROUTE TO MADNESS . . .

He led her on, tantalizing her with featherlight touches until she could stand no more. For all the imaginings that he had inspired, the moment was at hand. Overwhelmed by the strength of her own need, she threaded her fingers through the damp hair by his ears, pulling his head down until the kiss was complete. At her signal, he deepened it, parting her lips further with his own, gently caressing them, coaxing the response which had been so long denied yet waited, just below the surface, aching for expression . . .

D0596373

AMBER ENCHANTMENT

Bonnie Drake

A CANDLELIGHT ECSTASY ROMANCE™

Published by
Dell Publishing Co., Inc.
1 Dag Hammarskjold Plaza
New York, New York 10017

Dell ® TM 681510, Dell Publishing Co., Inc.
Candlelight Ecstasy Romance™ is a trademark of Dell
Publishing Co., Inc., New York, New York.

ISBN: 0–440–10842–X

Printed in the United States of America
First printing—December 1982

To Our Readers:

We have been delighted with your enthusiastic response to Candlelight Ecstasy Romances™, and we thank you for the interest you have shown in this exciting series.

In the upcoming months we will continue to present the distinctive sensuous love stories you have come to expect only from Ecstasy. We look forward to bringing you many more books from your favorite authors and also the very finest work from new authors of contemporary romantic fiction.

As always, we are striving to present the unique, absorbing love stories that you enjoy most—books that are more than ordinary romance.

Your suggestions and comments are always welcome. Please write to us at the address below.

Sincerely,

The Editors
Candlelight Romances
1 Dag Hammarskjold Plaza
New York, New York 10017

AMBER
ENCHANTMENT

CHAPTER ONE

"Strrrike!" The voice behind the mask delivered its loud verdict to a chorus of disbelieving gasps.

"But that was above his *shoulder!*" one high-muted chirp rang out.

Another echoed the sentiment in a barely disguised whisper. "*He* couldn't have hit *that!*"

Then came the third, its call louder and, more dangerously, directed at the offending umpire. "Hey, get your glasses—"

"That's enough, kids!" Amber MacLaine, clutching scorebook and pencil to her chest, stepped back from the baseline to still the team sitting on the bench. A sweeping flick of her wrist made a place for her in their midst. As she eased her slender frame down onto the hard wood, her tone held gentle warning. "Take it easy, now. Remember what I've told you—we win some, we lose some. Some calls go our way, some don't. Let's be patient. It'll even out."

"But, Mrs. MacLaine—"

"No 'buts,' Billy. Patience!" Her own stayed in check, as a jabbing forefinger returned the attention to the game. Some more begrudging than others, all eyes turned back to the pitcher's mound. Sensing that he was once more the center of attention, the young pitcher adjusted his visor lower to blot out the lengthening shards of early evening sun spilling over the field, pulled himself up to his full four-foot-seven height, executed his most sober windup, then released the ball. All eyes followed its progress as it faltered toward the plate, seeming to hover on the outside corner before tipping the edge of the catcher's mitt and bouncing into the screened enclosure behind.

"Strrrike!" *Close, perhaps justified this time,* she decided, glancing at the twelve boys and two girls to her right and left on the bench, raising a warning finger to her lips when rebellion appeared imminent then passed. A faint sigh of relief stole through her. It had been one thing to spend the last six weeks teaching these nine-year-olds the fundamentals of baseball, another to instill the attitude of good sportsmanship, her primary goal as a coach. A fighter herself, on more than one occasion it had taken every ounce of self-control to keep from yelling out her own opinion of the umpire's haphazard calls. Now, frustration on the rise, she bit her lip. Little Peter Solway, the batter, had been up on the count, with three balls pitched, until the last two strikes were called. The full count put on the pressure. It would be hard enough for him to connect with the ball under optimal conditions; his only realistic hope of reaching base was on a walk. Fingers crossed, Amber urged the child on silently. *Relax, Peter. You can do it.* A hit would be just what his faltering ego needed.

Once again, there was the somber ritual of the visor-pull, the windup, and the release. Once again, the batter stood motionless as the ball approached, then whizzed by at eye level. Once again, the catcher went scrambling into the corner after it. "Strrrike three!"

This time, Amber did join the protest. Young bodies jumped up and down excitedly as she bounded toward the plate, a length of long blond ponytail streaming out from above the adjustable band of her team's black hat. Long, slim legs, bare and delicately tanned from shorts to sneakers, covered the distance before the dejected boy even lowered his bat. "Good watching, Pete. You almost had it." Her warm words sent the little batter back to his teammates, as she moved on, calling calmly to the umpire. "Excuse me, a word, please!" Reluctant to argue blatantly in front of the children, she gestured him to join her several yards from home plate. "I'm not sure if we have the same definition of the strike zone here," she began carefully and in a lowered voice. The tapered fingers splayed at her hips emphasized their shapeliness. "That last one was way above his shoulder!"

The umpire's mask came off to reveal a thoroughly disinterested look. "Just about *at* his shoulder, ma'am," he corrected indolently, all but yawning his enthusiasm. Just a boy himself, in Amber's opinion, he looked no more than twenty-one. Not for the first time this season did she wonder where the league picked up its umpires. In the case of this particular call by this particular umpire, it was wrong. "*At* his shoulder?" Her voice contained as much of a squeal as its whispered timbre would allow. "At *whose* shoulder?" The pale green of her eyes suddenly flashed darker with the vehemence she tried so desperately to contain. "You seem to forget that these children's shoulders are considerably closer to the ground than yours!" The frustration of the season, a heartbreaker for her kids, had begun to take its toll, driving her on. "And that first strike you called was even higher!"

A carefree shrug met her accusation. "It was questionable—could have gone either way." His move to replace his mask and resume the game was halted by Amber's final plea.

"Either way?" Her eyes widened as she cried out incredulously, then instantly willed her voice to lower again. A slender finger shot out toward her now-scattered bench. "My poor kids are behind by eighteen runs. With only one inning to go, couldn't you give them even the slightest benefit of the doubt?" It had been the story of the season for the Pirates—runs against them, close calls against them, only a multitude of errors and their enduring spirit to their credit.

"I do my best, ma'am." His offering was devoid of feeling.

"That's not good enough!" Infuriated at his total lack of compassion, she whirled on her heel, instantly colliding head-on with the wall of warm humanity that had approached from behind during the exchange. Had it not been for the bracing fingers steadying her shoulders, she might have fallen on the rebound.

"Whoa, what's the problem?" His voice was deep and his head was held high. With a step back, Amber looked up determinedly at the newcomer. His own hat and dark glasses hid his expression, though his lips twitched at her resilience.

"That last pitch was *no* strike!" Her angry denunciation was met by an irrepressible grin, the inappropriateness of which prompted her follow-up. "And who are you?"

The man wore faded denims and an old crimson T-shirt with H-A-R-V-A-R-D emblazoned across its broad expanse. Now, a dark eyebrow shot skyward in open amusement. "It's *my* team that's creaming yours, little lady. I'd suggest you return to your bench . . ."

Rankled by his condescension, she pulled herself up straighter, appalled at her mere five-foot-six inches in comparison with his far greater height. "So *you're* the Cubs' coach. We're glad you could finally join us." Sweet sarcasm coated her words. "We waited as long as we could before one of the other parents took over." Cheeks flushed, she belted away, aware that there was enough of a spontaneous intermission in progress among the small players to permit her diversion. "Your team plays beautifully without you!"

Twirling once more, she made good her escape, simmering as she gathered her team around and approached the bench. The pep talk was of the type she had become expert at delivering, therapeutic in its way for her as well. With a softer word of additional encouragement to one of the players, she sent him to the plate.

For several plays, things looked up. One batter singled, then stole second when the catcher missed another high pitch. The next batter hit a fly ball toward second base, a breath stopper until the second baseman bobbled, then dropped it, at which point the Pirates had players on first and third. Amber cheered her heart out. "Come on, Eric. Eye on the ball. Nice and easy! Josh," her eager call carried to the boy on third, "don't run until you're sure." She cupped her hands toward first. "On your toes, Amy!" To lose by a score of eighteen to two, or three, or heaven help us, perhaps even four, would be better than the eighteen to nothing debacle glaring from the scoreboard now. Then, the inevitable happened.

An unintentional bunt—the ball somehow made contact with the bat to the hitter's shock, then belated delight —brought the third-base runner home. In a melange of arms and legs and dust and leather, a small white speck of ball grazed the runner's leg. "Out!" The umpire's decision tore all hope from the Pirates' universally rounded eyes. In a flash, Amber took the side of her team, rushing forward quickly.

"Did you *really* see that ball touch Josh *before* his foot reached the plate?" It was so cruel; her little players had struggled so to have the possibility of a run. "Are you *sure* it was an out?" When the umpire nodded complacently, she opened her mouth to argue further. A purposeful tug at the back of her head startled her into momentary silence. Allowing her no time to recover, the hand that had captured her swaying mane proceeded to guide her smoothly from the fray. Its pressure was playfully firm, calculated to move her without hurting. Though her scalp prickled at its hold, there was promise of a sting only if she demurred; she did not. On the more private realm of the sideline, she was released.

"Look, miss," he began, his eyes still hidden behind those darkest of sunglasses, his forehead by its low-drawn visor, "I realize that you're defending your team. But,

11

don't you think you should soft-pedal it a little?" The ease of his stance, legs planted firmly apart, one hand in his pocket, the other falling idly now by his side, spoke of supreme confidence.

Amber faced him indignantly. "You know, coach, if *you'd* sat back and watched the pounding *your* team had taken for the bulk of the season, you'd be incensed, too. It's been one arbitrary call after the other against my kids. From my viewpoint, that child reached the plate fully two or three seconds before the ball did. Do you disagree?"

He thought for a minute as a firm hand rubbed the back of his neck, then chose his words carefully, seemingly convinced of her good intent. "No, I think you may be right. But the umpire made the call, and it's up to us to stand by it. Isn't that what these children have to learn?"

The tingling at her scalp slowly faded beneath her one-handed massage. "Very painfully . . . yes. It's a shame the lesson can't be taught in a little more . . . gentle way, though." Her pointed words held dual meaning, not lost on the clearly masculine features before her.

His smile was softer this time, though the strong mouth and jaw were a giveaway to his character. Her eyes narrowed. "I can't help but wonder whether, had I been a father, that umpire might have called things differently." Had she been a father, she mused, she certainly would not have been hauled away by the hair, at the mercy of the opposing coach!

An uncanny sense that the eyes behind the glasses traveled her length in comment was fodder for her suspicion. "You certainly aren't a father," his deep voice drawled in humor. "Perhaps you should play on your inbred . . . talents . . . a little. Sugar is often more palatable, you know."

Amber didn't need his eyes to convey the track of his mind. "My God! You're as bad as that umpire. A chauvinist throwback, if I ever saw one! I'm surprised you even allow any girls on your team!"

12

As though beckoned by her words, a beautiful child-player with long dark hair flowing from the confines of her green baseball cap approached, sidling up close to her coach.

"Daddy?" she whispered urgently. "We're all waiting!"

The tall figure lowered his head to speak with infinite softness to his daughter. "Hold them off a minute longer, Liz. I'm just about done." The bold face held a smug grin when it returned to savor Amber's astonishment. "Not quite as much of a throwback as you had hoped, hmmmm?"

With a resurfacing of her own good sportsmanship, Amber acknowledged her error, mirroring his grin with her own, faintly sheepish, but soft and sincere. "You have my apology. And my compliments. She's a good little athlete."

A dark eyebrow edged over the upper rim of the sunglasses. "So you do know how to turn it on, after all."

The moment's truce was broken by her burgeoning defiance. "I don't have to 'turn it on,' as you so blithely put it, when it comes to honesty. Now, if you have no other hair-pulling to do, perhaps we should let the children continue?"

"By all means." His head angled slightly to the side. "I do believe this is *your* messenger coming now." The glasses reflected her own face once more before aiming again at the boy approaching. "The resemblance is remarkable. I must admit that you deserve credit for taking on your little brother's baseball team."

Amber nearly choked on a laugh, held back but barely as Scott drew even with them. "Hey, Mom, how about it?"

Turning, she lay a possessive arm across the boy's shoulder. "Sure thing, Scottie!" The triumphant glow cast quickly over her shoulder as she walked back to the bench with her son brought its own reward; the expression of astonishment, so akin to hers earlier, which eclipsed both cap and glasses on the face of the Cubs' coach, was worth

13

the few tingling reminders of his strong-arm tactics. It seemed that this time around, at least, she was to have the last laugh.

It was short-lived, however. The final score was a demoralizing twenty-one to nothing, the worst beating the team had taken yet. "Come on, guys! Ice cream cones are my treat!" she announced to the quiet group of discouraged players, after the obligatory handshake lineup had been completed.

"But, Mrs. MacLaine," one of the little girls, so prone to logic, piped up, "we *lost!* Ice cream cones are only for when we win!"

The spontaneous cheers which had sprung from the boys at Amber's suggestion threatened to turn into a roar of boos directed at their more practical teammate. Lifting both hands for silence, Amber reassured them. "As far as I'm concerned, you're *all* winners—the best sports any coach could ask for." She ruffled the several hatless heads within reach. "Besides," an impish grin played at her lips, "the ice cream is a bribe. We're having an extra practice at nine o'clock on Saturday morning. I want all of you to *be there!*" The refrain of boos would not be denied this time, but faded quickly in the dash toward the waiting wagons, leaving far behind the humiliating loss, letting a jimmy-covered ice-cream future beckon.

"Is that everything, Scottie?" she called from the base of the stairs, one hand tensely clutching the curved tail of the banister, a high-heeled foot on the bottommost step. A glance at her thin gold wristwatch told her that there was little more than ninety minutes to go before takeoff. With the airport a forty-minute drive away, they had but a few moments left at home together. Her already jumpy stomach lurched at the thought. "Scott?" The silence that echoed from the second floor drew her upward to pause only at the open door of her son's room. Two years of summer's partings made this third no easier.

14

The figure sat, small and forlorn, on the edge of the corduroy covered bed, staring blindly out the window at the lush maples in the yard. It was always like this—the last minutes. For the past few weeks, she had kept them both busy, running raggedly from one thing to another at the end of each school day, working late into each night in hopes of denying the inevitable anguish. Now, with classes adjourned just yesterday, all had been done. There was no more putting off the fact that, with the drive to the airport, her son would be gone to the West Coast for the summer.

Slowly, she walked toward the bed, a knot forming at her throat. Quietly, she sat down beside the sad form, gently wrapping her arms around him, gathering his special warmth to her. She had always taught him to cry freely, yet it was only in the protective cocoon of his mother's arms that he let go. His shoulders shook as silent tears slid down his cheeks.

"Shhhh," she crooned softly as she rocked him, her face buried in the thick thatch of sandy-brown hair. His tears were so innocent, those of a child leaving home and mother. Her own, now barely held in check, reflected the anticipation of separation from the one in life who was dearest to her, her very flesh and blood. To absorb his sadness, to feel what he felt compounded her own unhappiness.

Seconds meshed into minutes, the long hand and the short, much as their arms wound around each other, hers long, his shorter. These moments were too dear to be rushed, for they embodied the closeness of this mother-son relationship. The warmth of their mutual comfort would have to last them in memory through the summer.

Just when Amber's eyes had cleared, the low whispered "I love you, Mom" moistened them afresh. It was another stretch of time before she could begin to answer him.

"And I love you. Very, very much, Scottie. You know that, don't you?" The small head nodded against her blouse as she added, "I'll miss you."

15

"Mom"—he drew away to look at her—"why don't you come out to visit in a few weeks?"

Her fingers blotted his wet cheeks with a tenderness echoed by her eyes. "You know I can't do that, Scott. Your dad will keep you really busy, and there's your grandmother and grandfather. They've been dying to see you. And Aunt Sherry and Uncle Richard—"

"You still don't want to see him." The boy's hazel eyes, so like hers in shape and depth, challenged her, sending a knife thrust of guilt through her.

"It's *you* I'd want to see, but you'll be so busy that you really won't have the time." She lifted the backs of her fingers to brush at the moistness at the outer corners of her lids.

"What about you, Mom? What are you going to be doing while I'm there?"

Amber forced a tremulous smile to her lips in a half-hearted show of nonchalance. "Oh, I'll be writing. You know me, never without a pen in my hand."

The appearance of his small grin broke through the worst of the gloom. "Will you be here at the house most of the time?" Even as a child, he had been comforted by knowing exactly what her plans were, where she would be while he was in school, where she and Ron would be when they went out together. She often wondered if Scott followed her day in his mind, much as she did his.

"Ummm, some of the time I'll be here. I'll be at the hospital every morning, though. If there's any problem, you can reach me there. Any operator will give you the number of Massachusetts General, then all you have to do is to ask for the Public Relations office." The thought of this new job brought a brighter light to her liquid orbs, giving their pale green a semblance of sparkle. Scott immediately sensed her pleasure.

"You're excited about it, aren't you?"

"Uh-huh. It should be fun. I've never done PR work before. My writing has always been much more on a free-lance basis. This will be different—working on one project for the summer. But the nice thing *is* that it's only for the summer, while you're away. I'll be bored and waiting for you by the time you get back. Hey, have you got your camera packed?"

The boy's eyes rounded. "Oh, no, I almost forgot!"

"Well, don't forget," she teased gently. "If you and I are going to put together a summer diary, we'll need pictures. You've got your notebook, haven't you?" With Scott's dawning interest in photography, it had been a mutual brainstorm for him to keep a detailed log of his summer, both for his mother to see and for a keepsake at its end. It was one activity that would bind them together daily during the weeks apart.

"Yup. In my suitcase." His grin warmed her.

"Then, you go get the camera," she urged, standing and smoothing his hair back from his forehead, as though reluctant to relinquish even this small hold on him, "while I get myself put back together. I'll meet you downstairs."

Moments later, in the bathroom that adjoined her bedroom, she studied her somber image in the glass. Her tear-smudged makeup was a sight, though not much better than what lay beneath. The past few weeks had etched fine lines of tension around her mouth. The frequent late-night writing sessions had painted deep smudges beneath her eyes, whose hollowness was a reflection of her frame of mind.

Quickly repairing her makeup, she added concealer and blusher, then sighed, knowing she could do no better. All in all, she was certainly presentable. Despite her pallor, the finely sculpted lines of her face held a natural beauty, emphasized with poignancy by the neat draw-back of her blond hair into a low twist at the nape of the neck. She wore a soft white blouse, its buttons opened only far enough to preclude cleavage, the offering of lightly tanned throat boasting an exquisite gold chain to match the studs at her ears. Her skirt was navy and white, in a dirndl style, crisp yet feminine, hemmed just below the knees to reveal the length of browned leg below.

Returning to the bedroom, she straightened the waistband of her skirt, seemingly looser than it had been two weeks before, grabbed the white leather bag that matched her high-heeled sandals, extracted and applied a light pink gloss to her lips, then, with a sigh of resignation, headed downstairs to join her son.

The streets out of Dover had never been as beautiful, tree-lined and clothed in a magnificent array of summer greenery. An easterner by origin, Amber had missed these seasonal distinctions during her years in California. Her relocation to New England had already justified itself on this score—with the crispness and vibrance of fall, the chill and snow-filled air of winter, the bright and gay rebirth of spring, and, now, the warm richness of summer just bursting with pleasure.

On this sun-blessed day, the local streets were particularly quiet, instilled with the laziness of the newly arrived summer season. Dover was a peaceful town, as went the westerly suburbs of Boston. Its homes reflected the flavor of its residents—from the older, more stately to the younger, more contemporary. Its fields and meadows spoke of a countrified pace which its sophistication belied. For Amber and Scott, it was a comfortable and welcoming community, a perfect spot to make their home.

As the Dasher wagon passed unerringly through the maze of back streets toward the more open expanse of Route 128 and, then, the Massachusetts Turnpike, both its occupants were lost in their own thoughts. The boy's ran ahead, with trepidation, some three thousand miles across the country to his father and that "other" half of his life. The mother's ran back to the fateful decision of nearly four years past. Had it been the right one? she wondered anew. For herself, there was no question; without Ron, she was a happier, more confident person than she had been in years. For Scott, the question was more complex. Did

18

he miss the family unit that had existed, albeit merely as a formality, before the divorce? Did it bother him to spend nine months out of each year without a father? He was growing older, perhaps more in need now of such a masculine figure than he had been before. Could she be both mother and father, as she had so desperately tried to be since their move to Massachusetts?

A well of pride surged within her as she cast a glance toward her son's face. He was so handsome, so angelic— dressed to the hilt in his new Levi's jeans, new Lacoste jersey, and new Nikes—that it was hard, at this moment, to recall the many points of contention between them during the past years, all minor in hindsight and totally typical of a preadolescent. There were, for starters, fights about clothes. Scott's preferences ranged from the old to the torn to the faded; his mother's veered toward the well-kept. The boy shunned her preference for sweaters and jerseys in his bid for anything with either a slogan or a team number on it. And footwear—that was an issue in itself. Not only was he allergic to anything warm or leather, but the only sneakers permissible in his wardrobe were those with a dark blue stripe in vee-formation on the side. Amber had finally given in on the latter, so long as they were clean and in relatively one piece.

There were fights about food; Scott had an aversion to anything new or of the vegetable family. There were fights about bedtime; more than once, Amber had found a flashlight burning by his bedside, atop the latest issue of *Sports Illustrated.* And, yes, there were fights about reading—not that she pushed him toward anything really heavy, but she finally conceded that *some* reading was better than *none,* even if it was nothing more than the sports page or the latest space-age epic.

Finally, and most recently, there were fights about haircuts. Amber had long since learned to schedule them for the afternoon that school let out for vacation; that way, the schoolmates might fail to notice completely. There was nothing more desperately "the pits," her son informed her vehemently, than to look newly groomed. Amber recalled this now with a grin; give him another few years, she mused, and he'd change his tune!

The five-laned asphalt of the Massachusetts Turnpike skimmed beneath her wheels, cutting neatly through the west suburban towns skirting Boston. Parks and residential stretches gradually yielded to the heavily concrete landscaping of the urban character. This, too, she loved— the ability to move from country to city and back with such ease. For Boston harbored a wealth of offerings, many of which she had already sampled. Not only was it a world-famous medical center, but its educational community was equally renowned, housing such institutions as Harvard and M.I.T. In the culture department, the city had much to boast—its theater district, including the new Metropolitan Center, the Museum of Fine Arts and its Pei-designed West Wing, the Aquarium, the Museum of Transportation, and the Fogg Museum in nearby Cambridge. History flourished in the hub, kept alive by such timeless landmarks as *Old Ironsides*, the U.S.S. *Constitution*, the Paul Revere house in the North End, and the sites of the Boston Massacre and the Boston Tea Party. Then, of course, there were Lexington and Concord, Plymouth Rock, historic Salem—all an easy day's exploration. Amber smiled with pleasure as she recalled with satisfaction the many things she and Scott had discovered.

Pausing at a toll booth in Cambridge, she reached over to squeeze the boy's hand in encouragement. There would be many more fun times, she knew, come fall, when he was back from the Coast. Despite all their minor squabbles, Scott was a terrific kid. She was the first to proclaim it. He was well-mannered, a good student, and well-liked among his friends. The broad grin he shot her melted her heart, and she forced her eyes back to the road in self-defense against the emotion which lurked too close still for comfort.

"There's your park!" she teased him, as the high matrices of the lights of Fenway Park came into view on their right. "Will you be able to catch the Red Sox in Anaheim?"

"We did last summer. Dad's pretty good about getting tickets. But," he scrunched up his nose impishly, "I still like Fenway Park best. It's so cozy."

Amber chuckled. "It certainly is! But the Red Sox aren't doing so well this year. You might do better to root for the Angels."

"No way! Dad can cheer for the Angels—I'm with the Red Sox all the way!"

As he settled back in his seat and gazed out the window once more, her own thoughts wandered. The John Hancock tower loomed on their left, its windowpanes relatively intact at last. What a scandal that had been—for the insurance company to have invested hundreds of millions on their new skyscraper, only to find that the windows cracked and popped out at the slightest provocation!

Momentarily diverted, she wondered what had happened to the insurance executive from that same upstanding company, who had called her so many times last year. Somehow he hadn't been able to understand that she didn't want to date him. If only the disastrous original glass walls on that building had been half as thick as this one executive's skull!

On this day when she would have liked to linger, savoring each quiet moment with Scott, the traffic flowed smoothly. The Turnpike dumped them onto the Southeast Expressway, from which they easily connected to the tunnel beneath the harbor, then on to Logan International Airport. Tension slowly built a knot in Amber's stomach, aggravated by the sight of the huge birds, landing and taking off, beyond the terminal buildings. It was as though this world, which opened vistas to others, held a fast-closing door for her.

All too soon, she walked Scott aboard the plane, stowed

his bags, talked with the stewardess, then returned to his seat for the final farewell. Through the tears that welled at the backs of her eyes, she had to admire the child's fortitude. It was as if he had made his farewell back at home, in his room. Now he was fine, acclimated to the summer and to the temporary absence of his mother. It was, in some ways, an adventure, to fly from coast to coast each year. His instinct for rationalization was strong . . . particularly since he had no choice in the matter.

For Amber, things were not as easy. This was the last reality she would have envisioned when she and Ron had eloped so long ago. In the end, she, too, had had no choice. Yet, as she hugged the pliant child to her for a last, final moment, her whole being cried out that it should have been different.

Her throat ached, yet she needed these last words. "Be good, Scottie! I love you."

Her son's voice was soft, yet strong. "I love you, too, Mom. You have a good summer. You'll call, won't you?" For a split second, the world of doubts surfaced in his hazel gaze.

Amber smiled through her tears. "Every Sunday! Bye-bye, hon." Clutching at her pocketbook with fingers whose knuckles matched the leather's whiteness, she turned and left the plane slowly, blinded by a wall of tears to all else but the red carpet before her. Once in the passageway leading back to the terminal, she dug for a handkerchief, dabbed at her eyes, and continued on.

For what seemed an eternity, she stood at the floor-to-ceiling glass of the terminal window, watching, waiting for the plane to roll away from her. There were others on either side of her, engaged in similar vigils, yet she was oblivious to their plight. She stood at attention, hips resting against the wood guardrail at the window, one arm draped across her waist, the other bent at the elbow, its fist clutching the handkerchief to her tremulous lips. Had she been this way as a child, leaving for summer camp? It all seemed so very long ago.

Slowly the plane backed away, then taxied down the runway. Only when its wheels left the ground did she exhale the breath she had been unconsciously holding. Only then did the wave of fatigue engulf her. Suddenly weak in the knees, she put both hands on the railing for support.

"Are you all right?" The voice at her immediate left startled her, its deep resonance a breath of fresh air to bring her back to reality and the world which had to go on. She looked up quickly at the tall figure, then turned away again.

"Yes, I'm fine." The shallowness of her voice decried that claim.

The stranger continued to study her, almost analytically. "You look awfully pale. Are you sure you wouldn't rather sit down?"

There was something vaguely familiar in the fullness of his tone, yet she couldn't place its owner. "No, really, I'm fine." As if to assure herself, she released the guardrail, then reconsidered, when her knees turned to jelly. "On second thought, maybe I'd better."

Without another word, a firm hand took her elbow and guided her back to the row of bright blue seats several yards from the window. "Better?"

As she nodded, the tall figure slid into a chair beside her. In some strange way, his presence helped to ease the overwhelming emptiness she felt. Though his eyes continued to scrutinize her, he shunned conversation, sensing her need for none. Had she been watchful, she would have wondered at the puzzlement that flickered across his features as he searched for a crucial piece to an unfathomable jigsaw.

The activity of the airport swirled around them, lending muted accompaniment to their silence. Finally, she raised her lime-shaded eyes. "Thank you. I guess I was more tired than I thought. It's been a hectic few weeks."

Strong lips curved into a half-smile. "I know."

His voice held a conviction beyond mere conversationalism. He spoke from personal experience. Curiosity piqued by the welcome diversion, she studied him more closely. Dressed in a dark, three-piece business suit, a pale blue shirt, and striped tie, he was lean of hip and broad of shoulder. His hair was a dark brown, verging on black, full and tapered to the edge of his collar. An even tan spoke of hours of leisure in the sun, yet the intensity of his features belied a life of idleness. His jaw was as strong as the male lips firm; again, the sense of familiarity nagged at her. When her eyes lifted to his, the most royal of blues, the two pairs locked. In the instant, she realized she was staring.

A faint flush crept up to blend with the blusher on her cheeks. "I'm sorry. You look familiar, somehow."

Still holding her gaze, he smiled warmly. "I was thinking the same thing, yet I can't, for the life of me, place the face."

Embarrassed by the banality of the line, she dragged her eye back toward the window in time to see another huge jet, far in the distance, lift off the runway. Thoughts of Scott, now somewhere in the air headed west, filled her anew.

"Uh-oh, there you go again," the deep voice teased, "all misty and lonely-eyed." Only when he said it did she realize that her eyes had teared again. It would have to stop. Willing herself to regain composure, she looked down at the hands clutched in her lap.

"It's very . . . difficult."

"I know."

Again, there was that note of compassion from one who lived through similar emotions. Why did he *feel* so familiar? she asked herself once more. There was an intensity about him which struck deeply, but that was perhaps nothing more than a sign of her present vulnerability. An enigmatic force called forth her words.

"My son is on his way to spend the summer with his father." She heard her voice offer soft answer to his unspoken question, astonished at her lack of inhibition. She was not the type to open up to a total stranger like this. Yet, he didn't seem a stranger. Eyes still downcast, she sensed the force of his gaze on her. In her periphery, the shift of his body to corner in the chair and face her was clear. The strong hand which fell across a muscled thigh caught her eye, mesmerizing her with its confident pose. There was another, so like it, resting casually by a hip . . .

When finally he spoke, it was on an unmistakable note of triumph. "That's funny. I really *did* think he was your brother . . ."

CHAPTER TWO

Amber's eyes shot up in surprise to confront those that bathed her now in humor. Then, her pale brows lowered as she studied the face again. The hair and the eyes were new, very possibly hidden by a baseball cap and dark glasses. But the jaw and mouth—why hadn't she seen it before? As recognition dawned, a slow smile spread over her lips.

"Ahhhh," she drawled, "the coach."

His echo furthered her grin. "Ahhhh, the coach."

"Hmmph," she growled, recalling that horrible loss, "not much of one here, if her team loses by a score of twenty-one to nothing."

"Don't feel too sorry for yourself. My Cubs were on the wrong end of a similar score the game following that one. It seems that success went to their heads." His low chuckle was in harmony with hers. It was a harmless topic, its lightness in memory a perfect pick-me-up for her downed spirits.

"*We* didn't have that problem. Actually, we won our last three games. The other teams made more errors than we did." Her eye was drawn by another movement on the runway; this time it was less painful. As though sensing her thaw, he leaned forward.

"Say, would you like a cup of coffee? I didn't have much breakfast what with the hassle of getting here by ten thirty." Once more, there was a subtle hint that his day had begun with much the same agony as hers.

26

"I don't know," she smiled gently. "I don't usually come to the airport to be picked up by strange men. Can I trust you?"

"You know"—a dark brow arched, framing the deep blue of his eyes with a roguish cap—"if I hadn't recognized those lovely legs of yours, your spunk would have been an eventual giveaway. But you really looked ill a few minutes ago. I'd say you could use something to eat in addition to that coffee."

Strangely light-headed, she eyed him mockingly. "Sorry, I make it a point to avoid breakfasting with men, particularly married ones." A vision of the dark-haired child, his daughter, flitted through her mind.

"I'm divorced."

He was a magnificent man; how any woman in her right mind would have let him go was, at that moment, beyond her. But then, living with someone, day in day out, could hold many surprises; wasn't she the expert on those? No, handsome or not, she was better going her own way.

"Thanks, but I really should be getting back home—"

His voice softened dangerously. "Do you *enjoy* a big old house, made for a couple and kids, but suddenly ominously quiet?"

"And how do you know I live in a 'big old house'?" she asked defensively.

He didn't hesitate for a moment. "You live in Dover, don't you? At least, I did think that Little League was strictly an intratown ordeal. And, knowing the town as I do, the chances are"—his eye shot skyward in rough calculation—"nine out of ten that you live in a big old house."

"I do. And you're right." Again, her forthrightness surprised even her. "It *will* be horrid to return to."

"Breakfast?"

She nodded, settling something in her mind. "Yes, breakfast."

But the haunted cast which remained in her eye with

the thought of the emptiness awaiting prompted him to take her hand. She succumbed to the need, allowing herself to be drawn up beside him and falling into a slow and easy step. Even despite her high-heeled sandals, he towered gallantly above her. His gait bespoke the same confident air that his body exuded. For an instant, she conjured up the image of the denim-clad coach with his snug-molded crimson T-shirt.

"Did you go to Harvard?" she asked gently, as they walked. He dropped her hand to place his at the back of her waist, just lightly enough to guide her successfully around the corner to the coffee shop.

His grin held a hint of self-mockery, quite at variance with what she might have expected. "Of course."

He was very unlike those other Harvard men she had met during the three years she had lived in the area. Some she had met through work, others through local activities, still others through friends. She had dated none of them, yet several were exceedingly impressive. All had belonged to that smug fraternity of good looks, superior brainpower, and overblown egos. All . . . but this man. Yes, he had the looks, without a doubt. In that department, he did Harvard proud. Yet it appeared that he was either more modest than some, or simply able to take himself in stride. And regarding intellect, he was a mystery.

It was late for breakfast, early for lunch; the coffee shop was sparsely filled and pleasantly quiet. Seated at a table by the window, they studied their menus in silence until a sixth sense told Amber that she was once again the object of concentrated study. Lifting her eyes, she met his, bewildered by the mysterious expression they held.

"Is something wrong?" she whispered in mock secrecy, desirous only of lightening the brooding gaze. "You look as though my third eye is showing through my forehead."

It worked for a moment, bringing a brief chuckle from the depth of his throat. "No, nothing as dramatic as that. You look so different, though, than you did the day I saw you at the game." The ghost of his somberness prompted her to laugh.

"I don't *always* go around in shorts, a T-shirt, and a baseball hat!"

He smiled, relaxing. "You should. You looked great!"

The eyes that pierced his carried good-natured indignance. "That says a lot for the way I look now. I'll have you know that I spent a double session trying to make myself beautiful this morning."

"Between bouts of tears?"

His eye was far too sharp, his insight no less. Squirming, she looked away, relieved when the waitress approached for their order. His was a full breakfast of bacon, eggs, toast, and coffee; hers was an English muffin and coffee.

"Is that all you're going to eat?" he challenged softly. Disturbed by his persistence, she glared as she nodded at him. But he resumed his crusade the moment the waitress trotted off. "You could use a few more pounds. Even dressed the way you are, it's obvious that you've lost weight since I last saw you."

His audacity mushroomed in her mind as she realized that they had never even properly introduced themselves. "I'm sorry, I don't think I caught your name?" she asked with the sweetest of mockery.

"Zachary Wilder, champion of the woebegone, at your service." Sarcasm bounced off the thin slant of his lips, but when he opened his mouth to resume his harangue, he hesitated, sensing her fragile composure beneath her poised veneer. When he did speak, his voice was much more gentle. "It's taken a lot out of you. You look like you could use a week's sleep." His reference was obvious.

"Thaaaank you, doctor." With great effort, she bit back the multitude of indignant retorts in favor of one exaggerated drawl.

His self-conscious grin took her by surprise, as did the sudden diversion of his eyes toward the tableware before him. He was right—in everything he had said. Her sarcasm was an overreaction to the day, the weeks, the months past.

"I'm sorry," she offered softly. "It's just that I'm not used to having someone checking up on me. It's been a long time . . ." Her words trailed off before she said something maudlin. Besides, he understood. Suddenly, with that realization, she grew curious. "The schools in Dover ended for the summer just yesterday." Strong suspicion drove her on. "Is your daughter on that plane too?"

When he lifted his eyes, she caught their vulnerability. Yet, his voice was controlled and calm. "Yes. She's off to Chicago. Her mother and grandfather live there."

"Will she be gone for the entire summer?"

"Until the twentieth of August. Then she'll be all mine again." He smiled gently, sadly.

"It must be very hard for a man raising a daughter alone."

Their eyes met and his threw back a blue-shrouded question. "Is it any different for a woman raising a son alone?"

His point well taken, she sipped at her coffee, temporarily lost in thought. No, it was probably no different. Yet, her job permitted her the freedom to be a full-time mother, did his?

"What do you do for a living?" she asked on impulse.

His hesitation was brief but noticeable, then he broke into a easy grin. "I'm a doctor."

Memory of her earlier wit brought forth a lighter laugh. "So there *was* a method to your madness, then?"

"It was a personal observation, not a clinical one."

"Are you in private practice?"

He held her gaze expectantly. "No. I'm on the staff at the Mass. General."

So, fate might conspire to throw them together again, she mused silently. "Ah, the Harvard connection continued . . ."

She had taken it one step further; he grinned at her

30

acuity. "Yes, I do hold a position at the medical school. Obviously, you know something about the General."

Amber was fully appreciative of the caliber of doctor affiliated with the teaching hospital and its feeder university. In a city famed for its medical facilities, the Massachusetts General Hospital and Harvard Medical School were tops. And, yes, she was going to know even more about the two before the summer was out.

Grinning, she divulged her own nascent affiliation with the hospital. "I'll be there myself this summer."

Instant concern crossed his features, bemusing her. "Then you *are* ill?"

It took her a full minute to follow his thought back to the weak-kneed scene earlier. His misconception brought a soft laugh and a speedy denial to her lips.

"No, no. I'm fine. I'll be working there this summer. That's all!"

The face before her relaxed, rewarding her clarification with a devastatingly masculine smile. That he should have been so concerned about the health of a stranger mystified her, though she attributed it finally to his line of work. It took dedication to serve on the staff of a major hospital, as opposed to taking the more easygoing and lucrative road of the private practitioner. And the Mass. General was as demanding as they came, treating patients from all over the world.

"What, exactly, do you do?" His deep baritone rang into her thoughts.

"I'm a writer. I'll be working in the Public Relations department for the summer. They've got that new fund-raising project to launch; we'll be handling all of the literature relating to it."

The dark head nodded, its blue eyes suddenly distant, lost in thought. Then, as quickly, he returned. "What do you *usually* do—when you're not spending the summer doing PR work?"

"I free lance . . . wherever I can." Although she had

anticipated a struggle breaking into the ranks of Boston journalism, it had never materialized. Her friends in the area had seen to that, with her past credits backing up their efforts.

"What do you write?" His eyes left hers for a moment to acknowledge the arrival of the waitress with their orders.

Surprised to find herself actually hungry, Amber buttered her muffin and took a bite before answering. "Anything I get my hands on. Political pieces, personal interest stories—that type of thing."

"And your latest?" Could he guess, she wondered?

A sheepish grin spread from one small earlobe to the other. "I'll be doing a write-up of my experiences as a coach for the Little League team."

"So there's a method to *your* madness." He stole her line from her with a daring gleam in his eye.

Her chin tilted up defiantly. "I would have done it for Scott, anyway. My involvement seems to help ease the void."

"Does it?" His voice was soft and low, asking the same question that she had asked herself so often.

Eyes downcast, she let a silence ease the jolt of the dilemma. How could she tell what Scottie actually felt about it? From her own standpoint, it helped ease her guilt. She parried the matter with a shrug, looking back at him as she changed the course of the discussion.

"At any rate, *Boston* magazine will print the article if I write it. So, I write it!" Returning her attention to her breakfast, she missed the glint of respect which the mention of the publication brought to the face across from her. By the time she looked up, it was gone. "How long have you lived in Dover? Your accent tells me that you're not a native Bostonian."

"Nor yours." Having finished eating, he sat back in his chair to study her again. "Eight years. Four with wife, four without. How about you?"

"Three years. All alone." A pang of emptiness coursed through her, bringing an unknowing grimace to her gentled features. He took it in, then pondered it for long moments as they finished the last of their coffee and he motioned the waitress for the check.

"I've got to be getting back to the hospital. About a half day off during the week is all I'm allowed. Look," he grew more serious, "this day could be a tough one for you. And I'm not particularly looking forward to going back to an empty house, myself. Why don't I come by and take you out for dinner when I've finished at the hospital?"

Much as she had enjoyed the past hour—much as she had *needed* the past hour—Amber shook her head. "Thank you, but no. I'll have to get used to it, or the summer will be very long."

His head lowered more sternly, a swath of dark hair falling rakishly across his brow. "It's only as long as you choose to make it," he replied.

Again, she saw the truth to his words. Yet there were other, less dangerous things with which to fill her time. At a glance, this man was far too handsome, far too masculine, far too available for comfort.

"I'll keep busy." She spoke her thoughts aloud. "Besides, you don't even know my name. How can you ask me out?" The fact had jumped from mind to lips in a flash.

Had her resolve not been as strong, the dazzling smile he bestowed on her would have changed her mind about seeing him again. "I'll just call you 'coach.' Boy, did you look great in those shorts!"

Not knowing whether to be flattered or incensed, she merely shouldered her bag and stood. "Thank you for breakfast, Zachary. It certainly picked me up." Twirling on her heel, the only thing lacking was the long ponytail to snap for effect. The doctor was by her side before she even entered the long corridor.

"Where are you parked?" he asked, matching her brisk step easily. Amber willed her eyes to hold straight ahead.

33

"Right out front."

"*Right* out front? You *didn't* . . . !" He knew what was coming well before she did. It was only when they rounded the last corner and approached the main entrance that she saw the "man-in-blue," one of Boston's finest, very calmly and deliberately writing out a parking ticket.

"Hey, wait a minute . . . !" she yelled, breaking into a trot toward her car with a resurgence of the spunk that had fascinated Zachary Wilder once before. In her total preoccupation with this new predicament, she was oblivious to the dark-haired doctor who remained behind, hands on hips, grinning in delight. By the time she had finished pleading her case and had buckled herself safely into her car, the tall figure was gone. It was only after she had left the airport and had guided the Dasher through the Sumner Tunnel and back onto the Expressway that she realized how surprisingly pleasant a breakfast it had indeed been. Further, she had to acknowledge the success with which Zachary Wilder had taken her mind, for the time being at least, from Scott's departure. Unfortunately, it was an all too brief reprieve.

"And he actually gave me the ticket—while I stood there, reasoning my head off, trying to con him out of it! It was infuriating, Corey!" The telephone cord wound around the kitchen chair as Amber flitted in and out, wiping crumbs from the table, rearranging the flowers at its center, polishing an imagined dull spot on the varnished wood, all the time conversing with her friend.

"Amber, relax!" the gentle voice at the other end of the line urged. "At least Scottie got off okay, didn't he?"

A deep sigh halted her frenzied activity. "Yes, Scottie got off. He'll be there soon. I only hope Ron is right there to meet him." Her voice hardened. "He's so young to be traveling alone."

"It's done all the time, hon," Corey chided. "The airlines are expert at handling this type of thing. I'm sure there were other children on similar missions, flying on that very same plane."

Amber thought of Liz Wilder as she agreed, begrudgingly. "There were . . . but it's still a frightening thought."

"Look, Ron has always been there before, and he will be now. You and I know that's not what's really bothering you. Is it quiet there?"

Corey was Amber's best friend, her touchstone. "Deathly so! I've been stirring up as much of a racket as I can, but eventually I just wear out and then there's . . . nothing. Oh, Corey, did I do the right thing?"

"Yes, yes, yes! It's long since done, Amber! And, if you'd stop feeling sorry for yourself, you'd admit freely that it was for the best." Corey had known Amber and Ron as a couple; now she knew Amber alone. Without Ron, she was a person. "Your problem is that you harp on the past too much."

"Only with you, Corey. You know that. You're my best friend; I can tell you about all my little insecurities. Most of the time, I just accept them and plod on." From childhood, the two girls had been close, separated only during those years when Corey had attended medical school in the East, before Amber had joined her in the Boston area, divorced and with a son. Corey was married, though the demands of her career allowed no time for a pregnancy. Scott was her surrogate child.

"As you will do this summer," her friend continued the line of thought. "When do you begin work at—*that* place?"

Amber's lips curved widely at the other's emphasis. "Shame on you, Corey. Just because you're at Children's, yourself, there's no reason to begrudge me my fun. I'll only be ten minutes away!"

The easy laugh was shared. "I know, hon, but I wish you were going to be over here. Then I'd be able to meet you for lunch and all."

"Lunch? You mean, pediatric residents actually eat lunch?"

"Okay, okay. So we steal from the kids' trays when their backs are turned. But I do wish you were here."

Amber eased down into a chair, feeling herself begin to relax. "You've got Peter there. You don't need me for a luncheon rendezvous!"

At Corey's full guffaw, Amber conjured up the image of the stunning redhead dressed in white, attracting every eye around. "Peter's my husband! I see him for breakfast and dinner; why ever should I want to see him for lunch?"

"Uh-uh, you can't fool me, Corey. You adore the man —confess it!" Her voice had lowered with the dare.

The silence on the line was broken only by a tremulous hum of feigned debate. "Ach, I guess you're right. I do adore him. But you didn't answer my question." She deliberately shifted the crux of the discussion away from her own happiness. "When do you start work at the hospital?"

"Next Monday. Should be interesting."

"I'll say. But, listen, kid"—Corey's teasing held a note of reproof—"will you do me a favor and keep your eyes *open?*"

"Open? What are you talking about?"

"Just be on the lookout, all right?"

"For what?" Amber shrieked in amusement.

"*Men,* you dummy! Ugh, what am I going to do with you? You are impossible! There are some gorgeous doctors over there, even if they *are* at the wrong hospital!" Her voice held the singsong lure, despite its competitive edge.

But Amber would have no part of it. "Corey, you know I'm not interested."

"That's what you say now, but just keep an eye out, okay?"

"I certainly will not!" Her refusal was as exaggerated, in good fun, as the entire tone of the conversation. Corey was doing her best to divert her friend's mind, for a few moments at least, from the absence of her son. Recognizing this, Amber humored her by playing along. "I've sworn off men. For good! That's it!" Her shoulder cradled the receiver as her hands made the sweeping gesture that her words conveyed.

Corey wasn't to be put off as easily. "Look, I met this terrific guy a few weeks ago. You'd like him."

"No!"

"He's good-looking and brilliant."

"No!"

"Not even for dinner at our place? The men could always talk shop while we eat. Come on . . . what do you say?"

"No!"

Recognizing defeat, the redheaded pediatrician sighed. "You're a lost cause . . . but"—she perked up a final time—"you haven't heard the last from me, Amber. You've got the whole summer of free evenings, and I'll get you out at least once if it kills me!"

"It might." Amber grinned smugly, delighted at her own firmness.

A soft chuckle filtered over the line. "No pink flowers on my grave, then. They clash with my hair. Got that?"

"Got it! Oh, Corey—?"

"Yeeeeees . . . ?"

"Lunch at your cafeteria one day soon, just the two of us?"

"You're on. Talk with you later!"

The hand that replaced the receiver on its cradle was more steady than Amber had felt all day. She had much to be grateful for in this fine and loyal friend. And it *would* be fun to meet Corey for lunch. Actually, as she looked to the bright side, there were many things that would be fun to do this summer in New England. Perhaps . . . next week . . .

Idly, she stood and wandered through the empty house. Even after three years here, its charm was as strong as the first day she had seen it. Old and rather run-down, the price had been right, mortgage and all. Many of the repairs were things that she and Scott had been able to do together; others she had simply hired a local carpenter or plumber to do. All in all, the house was comfortable, roomy, and private, bounded on all sides by a miniforest of oaks and maples and pines, accessible only on the long paved drive that wound from the street. Though many of the neighboring homes had stables, the only riding she and Scott had gone in for was atop bicycles. Smiling to herself, she anticipated Scott's excitement when she presented him with his first ten-speed in August, when he returned home. Then they would *really* be able to do the long-distance biking they had always discussed so eagerly. The very thought of it brought waves of excitement to her, followed by swells of loneliness as she realized that it would be eight weeks before he did return.

The enthusiasm with which she fixed herself dinner was pitiful, second only to the interest she felt in the finished product. After picking and shoving the food around on her plate for a few minutes, she gave up all pretense of hunger, cleaning up the works and retreating to her study.

In a top corner of the second floor of the house, the room was her sanctuary. Lined with wall-to-wall bookshelves, her desk and its chair were its only pieces of furniture. The lighting was indirect and warm, though totally unnecessary now, with the evening sun streaming in through multipaned windows on both exposures. The article on Little League baseball—that was top on the agenda. Gathering the group of index cards on which she had already made preliminary notes, she shuffled them, sorted through, then rearranged them again. Pencil in hand, she put several fresh cards before her on the wooden surface. Her teeth bit into the pink eraser end, her eye wandered out the window. One bare foot traced the leg of the swivel chair. A shaped fingernail drummed softly on the pile of cards.

It seemed futile. All thoughts brought the image of

38

Scott to mind—Scott, flying by himself in that huge plane, having probably arrived by now on the West Coast, being reunited with his father. Aimlessly, her thoughts turned to Ron. They had thought themselves so very much in love. High school sweethearts, classmates, best friends—it had been Ron and Amber for as long as she could remember. But they were so young, so idealistic, so headstrong in their love. Both sets of parents had fought their plans to marry, so they eloped. Both sets of parents had told them to wait, but they had Scott. Then, both sets of parents stood helplessly by as the marriage fell apart, distraught yet supportive, and helpless all the same.

Amber thought of her parents, living in the same house in Maryland in which she had been raised. To this day they were supportive, despite their original opposition to her marriage. Yet, somehow, in light of the last, Amber had not been able to return there to settle with her son, following the dismal years in Santa Barbara with Ron. The defeat would have been an even more humiliating one, particularly when word got around—as it would inevitably have—about the reason for the divorce.

Disgusted with herself for the rehashing of this past torment, Amber threw down her pencil, bolted from the chair, and abandoned her project for a more amenable time. Sudden impatience with the silence drove her into Scott's room, where she snapped on his tape recorder and began to clean his closet. The identity of the music did not matter; habit told her it would be the works of either Blondie, the Cars, or the Who—any of which were loud enough and sufficiently senseless to drown out her depression. It was a yearly happening, this total room-cleaning once Scott had left. Usually spaced over the few days following his departure, her ministrations were thorough and merciless. The closet, containing toys, games, puzzles, comic books, old sneakers plus his wardrobe, bore the brunt of her frustration, as she threw out anything and everything that was too old, too worn, or simply too young for the more mature boy who would return at summer's end. That boy would hopefully have forgotten the detailed contents of his closet such that the pruning would be practically painless. Yet, for Amber this time around, the process of the pruning, itself, was far from painless. As she had done in her study, she discarded the project with a moan of disgust.

Restlessness haunted her as she roamed the house, unable to settle down to one of those tasks which was supposedly to fill her time this summer. Why the loneliness, the hollow feeling at the pit of her stomach, should be that much worse this year was a mystery to her. Yet it thwarted her every attempt at diversion.

On impulse, she headed for the garage behind the house, drawing out her new ten-speed and checking the wheels for air before hopping on it and pedaling down the drive toward the street. This type of exercise she had always enjoyed—hence, she had treated herself to a new bicycle on her last birthday. A quiet community such as Dover, relatively even in elevation with inclines well-spaced and gentle, was ideal for biking. In the past, she had admired the steady pace of the regulars who passed by her drive; now she might think to join their ranks. And, if she expected to keep up with her son at the end of the summer, she reasoned, it behooved her to work on endurance before he returned.

With yet an hour until sunset, there was plenty of light and a minimum of traffic on the roads through Dover. The last of the azaleas and rhododendron still splotched the roadside with great dabs of color, of pinks and purples, in harmony with the delicate white of the mountain laurel. The scent was pure country and divine. A gentle breeze played through the canopy of trees above, its soft tongue licked her skin much as a loving pet whose playmate was, for some mysterious reason, below par. Determinedly, she built up, then maintained, a rugged pace, feeling at odds with the leisure of the countryside, yet needful of expending the nervous energy. Ever so gradually, her tension

40

began to dissipate, caught up then scattered by the peacefulness all about. The blond silk of her hair, drawn up on either side into a firm-clasped barrette, streamed out behind as she rode. The whites of her sneakers cast their ever-rotating contrast against the darkened hue of the pavement. Long shadows fell across her path, creating visual tracks for her to follow.

Her narrow tires easily spanned the bridge over the Charles River, the very same ribbon of life that wound its slow and steady way into Boston and, at last, to the sea. Here in Dover, the water was clear and sparkling in the late day's sun. Ferns bowed along its banks much as did the young boy and his fishing pole further on down the shore. The rusticity of the setting added to its peace, bringing a glimmering smile to Amber's lips as she moved smoothly by.

Dover streets merged with Needham ones, which quickly and with verdant grace yielded to those of Wellesley. Five miles from home, now, Amber pedaled on, intent on total exhaustion and nothing less. The muscles of her thighs rippled gently as they moved up and down in rhythmic succession. Periodically, she straightened and flexed the firm line of her back, though never once significantly altering the pace. There was a freedom she felt, riding now with the wind in her hair, brushing her cheeks, buffeting her body. In a momentary surge, she was without a care in the world, a soft white dove, soaring high and free. Legs in constant motion, she whizzed on.

The stores of the center were open, attracting a lazy crawl of summer shoppers with its evening temptation. The faces were plain and honest, intelligent and old-world. Appreciative of their silent dignity, she pedaled on, toward the college grounds. As a large brown and gold sign signaled her arrival at the Wellesley College campus, Amber turned her bicycle onto its narrow paths, following the gentle undulation of the concrete deeper into the fountain of academia. Summer sessions had begun, scattering students over rolling lawns, before buildings, and on the shore of the small pond which shone gemlike in a miniature valley. It was here that she finally paused to rest.

Dismounting and lowering her kickstand, she sank onto the soft grass overlooking the pond. The all-encompassing serenity of the scene conspired with her weary muscles to entrance her. The sight of a young couple, arms enmeshed, feet dabbling at the edge of the water, turned her thoughts to those carefree days, just after she and Ron had married. They were students then, freshmen classmates at Stanford. Assuming themselves in love, they sat much as this couple did now, basking in the glow of their mutual attraction. What had really happened in the years to follow? she asked herself in bewilderment. More critically, *why* had it happened? Haunted by the same nagging fear, she found herself no closer to an acceptable answer now, four eventful years later. Disconcerted, she turned her head in escape toward the opposite bank of the pond. Inexplicably, her breath caught.

There, beside a late-flowering dogwood, stood a man. Tall and lean, decidedly rugged in contrast to the more delicate pink blossoms nearby, he returned her gaze unerringly over the distance of the water. Helmet in hand, his own bicycle rested not far from him. Dark glasses hid his eyes, a white headband held sweat-dampened locks of near-black hair from his forehead. His stance bespoke the same confidence she had seen that very morning in one Zachary Wilder. Instantly, her mind honed in on an image of him. It would certainly be too much of a coincidence to find him here—or would it? This was a well-traveled path, a bicycle path by description on the nearby posted sign. Indeed, her periphery took in a random smattering of other bikers. Yet this one held her gaze unremittingly. There was that same intensity about him, one which plunged into her very soul. It was hard to ignore.

Subconsciously chewing on the softness of her lower lip, she remained otherwise frozen. Did he come here often? Was it possible that, had she ventured out biking on other occasions, she would have encountered him before? Dover was a small town, as were, relatively, Needham and Wellesley. Was this his standard route?

If, indeed, the cyclist across the pond was Zachary, was he here for pure pleasure—or to combat a restlessness of his own? In the instant, she ruled out that probability. Certainly a man like Zachary Wilder was above such simplicity. Certainly, even after her own refusal of his company, he would have any number of women to choose from—women who would flock to his side on a moment's notice. But then, she mused, there was no real proof that this *was* the handsome doctor. And, if it were he, he made no sign of recognizing her.

Drawn compellingly by the dark figure dressed in white shorts, shirt, and sneakers, she sat for long moments without so much as a breath to dilute the potency of the visual exchange. If it were he, what was he doing here? If it were not, then what form of man held her so mesmerized? Fear of the silent force sent a shudder through her. In the end, it was the encroaching dusk that forced her to her feet and back onto her bicycle, sheer determination which kept her from looking back as she retraced her route off the campus and back through the streets toward Dover.

Much later that night, before sleep finally came, she was to ponder that apparition. There was something about Zachary Wilder, whom she had now twice encountered and felt sure to encounter again, that was magnetic and soul-reaching. Inexplicably, as though the specter on the hill had been an omen, she sensed him to be a future force in her life. It totally defied reason, this purely intuitive suspicion, yet it lingered in her consciousness long after she fell asleep that night, blessing her dream world with an obscure sense of excitement, of fulfillment, of contentment that had too long been absent. By morning it was all forgotten—but she felt more rested than she had in months.

CHAPTER THREE

The next few days were, as Amber had expected, characterized by mood swings from the energetic to the lazy, from the frivolous to the sober, from the enthused to the indifferent. Through it wound the thread of loneliness which she attributed to Scott's absence. By Sunday, however, when she put through her call to Santa Barbara, then managed to chat brightly with her son, free of the tightness of throat and the moistness of eye that had besieged her earlier that week, she knew she was fine.

Monday morning found her firmly entrenched in a chair in the office of the Director of Public Relations for the Massachusetts General Hospital. Tony Leeter was friendly and forthright, slightly bullish but abundantly sharp where his field was concerned. For several hours, the two of them pored over the rough information that had been gathered on the fund-raising project. The goal was a noble one—the establishment of an International Center for Sports Medicine to be housed at the Mass. General. Inevitably costly, the project entailed the raising of many, many millions of dollars to finance both the construction of a new and modern complex and the technical link-up with the foreign countries involved, a number growing by the month.

Arms loaded with more background material, Amber left the hospital shortly after one, heading home to begin wading through the pile. The subject fascinated her, sports-conscious as she was herself. Though many of her friends were runners, she had opted for the more strategic game of tennis, which she played faithfully two afternoons a week year-round. The legacy of sore muscles left by her evening bike ride had jolted her complacency as to her own physical condition, a situation she hoped to remedy as the summer progressed.

With the easing of that soreness, the evening outing became a regular thing. At first limited to the more familiar and immediate environs of her own neighborhood, it was a week before she ventured to the college again. Was it the beauty and serenity that had drawn her there? Or was it the thought of facing that shaded figure across the pond? Whether it had, indeed, been Zachary Wilder, she didn't know. The man did not return a second time. In the meanwhile, however, she had another occasion to come across the doctor.

The course of her research on sports medicine had taken her back through the years to the earliest clinics, both abroad and in the United States. The past five years had seen the legitimization of such departments at most of the leading medical centers in the country. The projected effort at the General would serve to pool the finest resources in an offering of diagnosis, treatment, and prevention of sports-related ailments.

It was in an article from the annual report of a competing Boston hospital that she first saw the name—Dr. Zachary Wilder, Chief of Orthopedics. Described as a brilliant doctor and, at age thirty-four, the youngest ever to hold that position in the hospital's history, his achievements in the field were impressive. Even five years ago, at the time of the publication of this annual report, his list of clinical studies and journalistic contributions boggled the eye, no less the mind. It was a well-earned jump he made across town to the General two years later.

Now, as she thumbed through the more recent information, it appeared that the erstwhile coach of Little League was not only a leader in his field, but the director-apparent

45

of the new International Center. *Impressive,* she acknowledged with a sigh of admiration, as she let her eye wander from the paper before her to the window, opened now to invite the warm summer's breeze into her study. The richly leaved grove beyond was a luxuriant backdrop for the image that materialized in her mind. Strangely, it was neither that of the jean-clad coach nor that of the proper-suited doctor. Rather, it was of the cyclist, dark and muscular, skin coated with a fine film of sweat, eyes holding hers magically.

It was clear to Amber from the start that an interview with the eminent Dr. Wilder would be a must for her work. When Tony proposed it the following morning, on her second day at the hospital, she was mildly unsettled. In normal circumstances, she would have had no hesitation. Through her other free-lance endeavors, there had been interviews with many an illustrious personality. As an interviewer and investigative journalist, she held her own.

Yet, in her mind, Zachary Wilder was not the "normal circumstance" to which she was accustomed. There was that all-seeing something in his subtle manner which disconcerted her. And there was that vague reaction within her at the mention of his name, a reaction which perplexed her. In the end, reason won out. He was handsome and friendly, a natural attraction; once recognized, she accepted those qualities. As an interviewee, he was sure to be open and easygoing. And, most important, the information he could give her, the quotes she might glean from the interview, would all be critical to the campaign.

Smothering her intuitive unease in a blanket of reasoned determination, she set up an appointment, through his secretary, for late Thursday morning in his office. Leaving her name and the PR department as identification, it occurred to her that he might not make the connection beforehand. After all, he didn't know her name. A soft laugh tinkled into the quiet of her small office-cubby. Perhaps she should have identified herself as "the coach"—that would have given the secretary food for thought!

That she spent a longer time dressing on Thursday morning became apparent to her only when she walked into the office to find the others already diligently at work. They seemed to accept her khaki suit as standard professional wear, its straight skirt and tailored blazer conveying an air of competency, softened only by the warmer pink fabric of her blouse. Her hair was pulled back into a bun, as she preferred it for work, and the flush on her cheeks was, for once, a natural one. Shortly before the appointed hour, she escaped to the ladies' room to freshen up her makeup, adding a second layer of mascara, a dab of powder, and a light lip gloss, before smiling in rehearsal at her reflection.

"Go get him, Amber," she murmured through gritted teeth. Straightening her shoulders, she willed herself to calmness as she started down the hall, wondering exactly what she was out to get as she entered the orthopedic unit and presented herself at the desk whose sign read "Dr. Zachary Wilder." Moments later, she found herself in a small and modest office, simply decorated with a handful of framed diplomas, generously shelved with the latest medical journals in the field, and neat and orderly, much as she had expected it would be.

"Dr. Wilder has been momentarily held up in the OR. He should be arriving shortly. Do you have something to read while you wait?"

That she had been escorted into his office to wait was a surprise, one which she finally attributed to the fact that she was, in her way, a member of the hospital staff. "Oh, yes, I've got plenty to read." With a grin, she lifted the folders in her arm, some of which contained background information, others of which contained her notes as to what she wanted to ask during this interview. "I'll be fine."

"Coffee?" the attractive secretary continued solicitously. Amber was quick to note the narrow wedding band and its matching engagement ring on the young woman's finger; unaccountably, she felt relieved.

"No, thank you. Another cup and I'll begin to shake. No, I'll just sit and go over my notes."

Smiling her understanding, the woman returned to her desk, leaving the office door opened and Amber to her musings. What was it like working for him? she wondered idly, her eye traveling the circuit of the room, pausing every so often to admire what appeared to be momentos of one address or another he had delivered. Her attention finally came full circle to rest on the desk, a modern teak piece covered with a deep blue blotter and numerous stacked folders and piles of papers. There were no truly personal items here, save the one small, chrome-framed photograph of his daughter, Liz, which stood on the edge of an adjoining bookshelf. Was his life this summer, bachelor rather than parent, full of the carefree social behavior to be expected of such a prime masculine specimen? Needless to say, he would have his choice of the nursing staff here at the hospital; perhaps there was even a female resident, with the smashing looks of her friend Corey, on his string. And Boston had its share of beautiful women, totally aside from the medical profession; Amber had herself felt far from glamorous, on more than one occasion, when she had shopped along Newbury Street and found herself side by side with the cream of the crop. "Banned in Boston" certainly did not apply to this attractive and socially graced group of women. Unconsciously, she checked to make sure that the buttons of her blouse were in place and the folds of her skirt smoothed out. Nervously, she twirled the gold stud in her ear, wondering all the while why she was on edge. When the sound of footsteps merged with the steady beat of the typewriter outside the office door, her pulse hammered in time.

"Heeeeeyyyyy, coach!" He stood at the door, all smiles and crispness and good looks, surveying her broadly

48

before entering the room and closing the door behind him. "How are you?"

Amber's heart accelerated at the sight of the man who now stood propped against the door, arms folded across his chest. For a minute, she was strangely tongue-tied, until his maddeningly confident grin goaded her into speech.

"You're looking very pleased with yourself. Is it because you're *only* ten minutes late?" Delighted to see him again, she could not restrain the smile that spread over her lips, giving jest to her words.

To her chagrin, he took them more seriously than she had intended, checking his watch and shaking his head in frustration. "I'm sorry about that. The surgery was more difficult than I expected. Actually, it's a lucky thing I *was* only ten minutes late. I rushed like hell to get cleaned up afterwards." The smile he gave her as he crossed the small space to perch on the corner of his desk was relaxed once more, as though he had, in that instant, put the surgical delay far behind and could now proceed to the next order of business. For Amber, *that* was a thorough analysis of the figure before her. He wore the traditional white coat of the doctor, yet it fit his broad shoulders and tapered torso with more dash than many a hospital corridor had seen in years. His pants were light gray, belted in fine black leather. The stark whiteness of his shirt was broken by a maroon and gray striped silk tie, knotted to perfection. He looked fresh and clean, his dark, dark hair still damp from his shower. For a brief instant, the image of the Wellesley cyclist superimposed itself, until she dispelled it with an imperceptible head shake and a gasp of determination.

The knowing gleam in Zachary's eye said that he had not been ignorant of her inspection—nor did he sit idly by during its progress. Had Amber's eyes been his, she would have observed a beautiful woman, much more rested this time than before, though still with the same ghostly sheen at the back of clear green orbs. The slight frown that

49

momentarily shaded his features disappeared when he spoke, deeply and with a velvet smoothness to his timbre that sent rivulets of excitement through her.

"How have you been?" he repeated, with subtle stress to the query.

Amber smiled in a determined show of strength. "I'm fine. There were several tough days, but it's . . . better now."

"Keeping busy?"

"Uh-huh." Confronted by the force of his royal blue eyes, she felt suddenly shy and nearly forgetful of her purpose. This was, after all, a business meeting, she chided herself. Zachary Wilder had enough to do without carrying on small talk with her. As though reading her mind and the urgency she struggled to recall, he prompted her.

"What can I do for you?" His voice was deep and warm, a rich melody which could have been distracting had she not had notes directly in front of her.

"I just wanted to ask you a few questions. We're going to put several preliminary flyers together and we'd like to be able to use some quotes." She reached down to the foot of the chair, where she had deposited her pocketbook and a small tape recorder. An identical one sat on the corner of Zachary's desk; both were evidently of hospital stock. "Do you mind if I record our talk?" It was a formality to ask his permission; she knew that he would have no objection.

He grinned mischievously, spreading a tanned hand on the thigh that rested on the desk. Its muscular strength molded his pants well. "No—as long as I get royalties on anything that hits the top ten." As she laughed easily with him, Amber felt her tension begin to recede. He put her at ease, as he had obviously intended. Without doubt, this man could do most anything he set his mind to do; that knowledge was a source both of solace and disturbance to her, though she willed all thought of the latter to a later time.

50

"Tell me about the project. Did *you* originate the concept of an International Center for Sports Medicine?"

"No. It's actually been around for some time. But conceiving of something as far-reaching as this is very different from seeing it become reality. I've been very active in this latest thrust, but I am only one of many." He paused, studying her keenly. "You look much better now. You must be sleeping."

Stunned by the abruptness of his change of topic, she stared at him. He had switched from business to personal without batting an eyelash; would he return as easily?

"Yes, ah, I am." She cleared her throat, musing that *he* might be more successful at that than she. The long legs, stretched casually to the floor and crossed at the ankles, were far too close for rational thought, as were the strong fingers, splayed now on either side of his lean hips, against the edge of the desk. Determinedly, she lowered her eyes to her notes. "I know that . . . there are many . . . individual sports clinics." Praying that he would interpret her faltering as contemplation, she struggled to clear her mind of all else but the interview. "What do you feel the International Center will offer, above and beyond the present offerings of these smaller centers?" Sure enough, when she dared raise her eyes, he was once again the pensive administrator. And mercifully, he seemed unaware of her meanderings.

A fluid movement took him from the desk to the window, where he stood for several absorbed moments before turning the slow blue beam of his gaze on her. "The advantages of pooled resources are many and phenomenal. For one thing, the best of facilities will be available to the largest potential population. For another, the most tested theories, the latest techniques will likewise be more widely offered. And finally, and most important, the best minds will have access to one another, forming a medical entity far superior to anything we have today." When he paused, she steeled herself for another personal foray, the force of his expression bearing directly into her. But his intensity was, this time, of a more global type. "There is an additional benefit, which I hesitate to mention for fear of sounding terribly pompous." If it was her encouragement he sought, she gave it freely.

"*Nothing* related to this project can possibly be considered pompous," she chided gently. "It's a fantastic enterprise; one can only admire it." Her soft smile spoke with the sincerity he needed.

"There has to be a political benefit from a project such as this. Oh, I don't mean just for our country, though we will certainly be seen as one of the leaders, particularly when the center itself will be located on American soil. But worldwide—" As he paused for breath, she marveled at the genuine excitement uplifting his features. "There are, today, too few ties uniting countries. We seem to be necessarily in a period of semi-isolationism. The International Center will be one small safeguard against total insulation and utter isolation—do I make sense?" It wasn't just idle inquiry; the depth of his gaze, blue as the deepest of waters in the seven seas, demanded an answer.

Enraptured by his dedication to the cause and its offshoots, Amber beamed her pleasure. "You certainly do. I tend to be cynical when it comes to beautiful pictures of world peace. But you have taken a very small segment of mankind and offered it something to bind its tie. You definitely have a point."

"Have you spoken to Scott?" The light in his eyes did not alter as he startled her again. The tumble from the idealistic high rendered her speechless, more so than the touching mention of her son. As she stared at him wide-eyed, it occurred to her that he had remembered the child's name, which by rights meant nothing to him. It was a lovely gesture, one that gentled her shock.

"Uh, yes," she stammered softly. "I spoke with him Sunday. He sounded . . . very happy." She thought for a moment, then added on wry impulse, "I'm not sure whether to be relieved or angry." Instantly, guilt surged over her. To have felt this way was bad enough; to express it to another was even worse. What would he think of her now? And, despite all arguments to the contrary, it *did* matter to her. Averting her eyes, she absently rubbed a forefinger across the corner of the recorder in her lap.

Admiring her honesty, he sensed her guilt. "I know what you mean," he began, softly and smoothly, not at all judgmentally. "It's very common, I'm told. Elizabeth enjoys seeing her mother and her grandfather—one part of me rebels against that. As the summer wears on, though, the novelty of her visit with them wears off. Then, I eat my heart out at the thought that she is all miserable and weepy, wanting to come home, when the court says that she can't for another three weeks."

Amber had never discussed these feelings with anyone. Yet, obviously, Zachary shared them. It was gratifying, as her quiet smile signified. "You've heard from Liz?" she asked timidly, unsure as to how much more he might open up.

He moved gracefully to the chair behind his desk, easing himself down before answering with a sigh. "Yes. Monday night. She sounds well." His dark brows dipped at the memory of that phone conversation and the emptiness he had felt afterward. But there was absolutely nothing he could do to remedy that void, at least where his daughter was concerned. The blue gaze which lifted to Amber's was suddenly wiped clean. "Do you enjoy your work here?"

Though he hadn't intended it as such, it was a vivid reminder to her of her purpose. "So far, it's been very interesting."

"And the article on Little League?" A spark of amusement lurked both at the corner of his eye and his mouth. That would be quite some article, he sensed strongly, having had a sample of the force of the young woman herself.

She was once again startled—and duly pleased—that he had remembered this other bit of information she had offered at their last meeting. But had that airport breakfast been their last meeting? Once again, she pictured the lone cyclist across the pond from her at Wellesley; once again, she banished the thought determinedly. "It's coming along—slowly. I purposely avoided it until I got used to Scott's absence, and now that I have, it's finally moving."

The buzzer of his telephone sounded loudly. Without releasing her eyehold, he reached to answer it. "No, Cheryl. Why don't you take a message. I'll get back to him in a half hour or so. And, please hold all other calls for now." The receiver touched its cradle with a thud, reminding Amber that time was, indeed, limited. Reaching into the abyss of her large pocketbook, she withdrew her camera. Then, at Zachary's surprised expression, she hurried to explain.

"Do you mind? I'd like to take a few pictures while we talk. It saves having to send another photographer around to bother you."

"Oh, it's fine," he drawled softly. "I'm just amazed at the extent of your talents." His mind had flown to a world of other talents, which the eye on the warm tremor of her lips hinted at. As though squirming beneath his touch, she shifted position in her chair, crossing one shapely leg over the other, glancing at her notes as she automatically cocked the shutter of the camera.

"Now, can you give me more of the details of the proposed center—facilities and equipment you will need?"

Her question was promptly ignored. "How long have you been photographing?" His lean frame lounged back in his seat, his hands joined at the fingertips, thoughtfully, in front of him.

Disconcerted by his gaze, she answered as quickly as she could, intent on returning to her original question. "Since I was a child. Now, about those facilities—"

A dark eyebrow challenged her. "With a Nikon? No

child uses a Nikon. Only the serious photographer, if not the professional, spends that kind of money . . . unless . . ."—he smirked wickedly—". . . you are a very wealthy lady."

"Of course not," Amber denied quickly, then sought to explain. "I've been working seriously with a camera for the past five years. I was given the Nikon as a . . . gift." An anniversary gift . . . her last . . . from Ron. Stifling a grimace, she continued. "Photography seemed to make sense—for situations precisely like this. If I can take the pictures myself at the time of an interview, much time is saved. And my free-lance offerings are that much richer with accompanying photographs."

Zachary studied her closely for a long moment, then baited her. "I would have thought you might have a handsome young photographer at your disposal. You know, the stereotypically virile and ruggedly good-looking type" —humor intermixed with an enigmatic expression as he finished—"who would be more than happy to tag along after you. No?"

"No!" By some miracle, her voice was dispassionate. Sensing his direction she wanted no part of any such discussion.

But the roles seemed suddenly to have been reversed, with Zachary now the interviewer. "Do you dislike men?"

"Of course not! Some of my best friends are men." The pale green of her eyes flashed sharply. "Is there some reason why I should despair of the bunch just because I was unfortunate enough to land the rotten apple?"

With a gasp, Amber realized the bitterness of her outcry. With a convulsive swallow, she wondered what had ever spurred her to express something that had been tethered for so long. Quickly averting her eyes from those sharply scrutinizing ones, she missed the momentary tensing of his jaw, then its subsequent softening.

"I'm sorry. I didn't mean to upset you," he began quietly. "It's just that you do seem to take a huge load on your own shoulders."

"I really haven't any choice, have I?" she answered softly, her statement clearly self-directed. "Things have to be done in the most efficient and productive manner. Therefore"—she sighed, took a deep breath, and raised her eyes to his—"I take my own pictures."

They had come full circle. Amber straightened her shoulders, her poise once more intact. Sensing this, Zachary finally opted to address her original query. "About those facilities we've proposed . . ."

For the next ten minutes, he competently outlined, for benefit of her recorder, the center's overall needs. The neutrality of the topic barely countered the magnificence of the face in her viewfinder. With all else falling outside the frame, the force of his features constricted her breathing. Click, whir; click, whir. Shot after shot she exposed, hardly hearing his words, intent only on the blue-eyed gaze that was magnified in intensity by the multiple element of her lens. His masculine appeal mesmerized her, as did the pride and dedication he exuded as he discussed this topic on which he was the authority. When she finally lowered the camera, it was because her own circuits were overloaded and desperately in need of a break. This man affected her in very strange ways—ways that no other man had done, since her marriage had ended so disastrously. In the four years from the time the decision to divorce had been reached, the idea of a serious involvement had not tempted her in the least. Yes, she did indeed have her share of male friends and acquaintances scattered here and there, but she had rarely sought little more than an interesting talk or a good laugh. On an occasion or two these relationships had verged upon intimacy, but Amber had always been able to back away. No man had inspired a hint of the deep, overwhelming passion she now felt. Sucking in her breath sharply as she bent to replace the camera in her bag, she wondered what it might be like to be with Zachary, to feel the weight of his arms around her and know the pressure of those strongly male lips against her own. Eyes downcast, she hid from him the sensuous light that flickered beneath their lids, concentrating instead on the tape recorder, until she felt her composure reestablished. With the dying off of his final sentence, she snapped the recorder onto STOP.

"How'd I do?" he beamed, threatening her poise anew as he flipped from impressive to endearing with the blink of an eye. He seemed so boyish at that instant, this man whose hands held such power, whose mind did likewise, and whose position at the hospital served to bind the two together with awesome potency.

"Just fine. And, thank you," she acknowledged, almost shyly. "You've given me a lot to work with. It'll take me awhile to go through all of this. If I have any further questions, I'll get back to you." Struggling to gather her belongings in her arms, she stood awkwardly and turned toward the door. In a breath's moment, he was by her side, deftly relieving her of the folders and recorder, much as a schoolboy would her books. A subtle thrill jolted through her, accentuated by the hand that settled ever so lightly against her back to ease her through the door, which he had miraculously managed to open.

It seemed a perfect time, had he been so inclined, for him to make mention of seeing her again. Yet, they walked toward the elevator in overwhelming silence, their eyes focused forward. His tanned forefinger pressed the button, and they waited, standing side by side, until the whir of the elevator announced its approach. For a brief moment, Amber became conscious of the racing of her pulse in response to the presence of the well-muscled form beside her. On impulse, she indulged her senses for the fast-fleeting instant. Above the sterile odor of the hospital itself, came the very subtle scent of soap and aftershave, a heady combination to newly awakening senses. When the door of the elevator quietly slid open, she felt the needed relief from this sensory build-up. He returned her things to her carefully, then, in a breathtaking moment for her, drew her closer, until their bodies nearly touched. His lips fanned her hair, his breath carried his soft words privately to her. She held herself in taut expectancy, willing her legs to give her support.

"Don't ever let me see you biking again without a helmet, Amber. It's unsafe."

The firm hand that guided her into the elevator gave her no time to recover from the shock of his words. The elevator door slid shut, breaking the connection, before she had even exhaled the breath she subconsciously held. Mercifully, another of the elevator's passengers had punched her floor; otherwise, she might have ridden the full circle once over. Dazed, she stepped off and hurried to her office, only there collapsing into a chair and analyzing her reaction to this totally unexpected finale.

First, it was clear that he did know her name, though he had avoided its use throughout the interview. And the fact that she had merely left the name of "Mrs. MacLaine" with the secretary when she had made the original appointment indicated that he had done some research of his own.

Second, it appeared that she had been right. It *had* been Zachary, by his bicycle, on the opposite shore. Even now, the memory of that image—so primitive and earthy, in a beautiful sort of way—sent a tremor of excitement through her. He had recognized her, as of course he would, dressed so much like the hotheaded coach of their very first encounter.

But although these first two facets of her reaction were positive ones, the third was not. Much as she fought it, the overwhelming sentiment which carried her out to her car and back home that afternoon was disappointment. He hadn't asked to see her again. She had held her breath, awaiting his move, but he had failed to make the one she had expected. In his office, he had been every bit as warm and open and interested as he had been that day at the airport—yet he hadn't offered a repeat of his invitation. What bothered her even more, if that was possible, was that she had *wanted* him to! Having refused dates right and left for the past three years, she had actually wanted this one. It was a new—and dangerous—thought to get used to. Had Zachary asked her out, she would have been helpless to refuse. And the further complication to her life that might have caused was hard to imagine. She had an unhappy marriage behind her, a son and a career before her. What place would involvement with a man as thoroughly appealing as Zachary Wilder have in that scheme? Frightened by the new and unbidden responses his presence had succeeded in evoking, she mused her gratitude that he hadn't asked her out. It was safer this way—certainly not as wild or carefree, but, then, those days were over and safety, sanity, and structure were what she and Scott needed.

"Amber! You look great!" The round-bellied man rose from his seat, offering both hands to her as she approached the table.

"It's good to see you, David." Indulgently, she offered a lightly tanned cheek for his kiss, then slid into the chair which the tuxedo-garbed maitre d' held for her. Smiling all the while, David Brigham gave a subconscious tug at the well-tailored jacket of his suit as he reclaimed the seat opposite hers.

"You're looking wonderful, Amber! Much better than the last time I saw you. We were all very concerned! And—I'm glad you finally agreed to let me take you out somewhere," he chided, lowering his bushy gray eyebrows in mild reproach. "It's not good to be that much of a hermit, you know."

Her eye skirted the room—taking in the elegant white linen and fine china setting on the tables, the unobtrusively diligent scurry of waiter, wine steward, and busboy alike, the aura of class and quiet dignity exuded by the other diners—before coming to rest on the ruddy-faced gentleman on whose ample lap she remembered sitting as a child. "Hmmm," she teased, "if I'd known you were offering Locke-Ober's, I would have taken you up on it sooner. This is a special treat—surpassed, of course, only by your company." Her eyes softened as she smiled, and her long fingers clasped the rounder ones of her host in a warm squeeze.

"Anything for Meg and Albert's little girl," he teased her affectionately, then shook his head in amazement. "You really were a wild bundle of spirit as a child. My friends had their hands full with you, my dear! But it seems that Father Time was the only one who could tame you after all. You've grown into a very mature and beautiful young woman, Amber."

Amber's blush preceded her playful growl. "Flattery will get you everywhere, my friend." Then, she sobered. "But I'm certainly not a little girl anymore—and I've got a very grown-up nine-year-old son to prove it."

One of the delightful things about David Brigham, from Amber's viewpoint, was that he knew just about everything about her and Scott. As an old family friend, a college crony of her father's, he had handled Amber's divorce when she moved to Boston. As a prominent divorce attorney in the area, he also knew of the emotional stress faced by many a divorcée. She could relax and be herself with him, knowing that he would understand her well.

"You just don't age, though, Amber—regardless of what you may claim." His clear brown eyes enveloped the woman before him, admiring her anew. Dressed in a simple lime-hued sheath, her hair clasped above either ear by an enameled comb and flowing down over her shoulders, her face practically bare of makeup but beautiful and healthy, she was the very image of youth. He sighed good-naturedly. "To look at you, I'd say you're all of twenty-

60

two. Now how did a twenty-two-year-old swing a nine-year-old son?"

Amber's face lit up with her grin. "You always *were* good for my ego, David Brigham, but I can see right through you. You know as well as I do that I'll be twenty-nine on my next birthday."

A dismissing wave heralded his words. "Well, no matter. You still look fabulous. Your parents will be glad to hear it—I have to call them tomorrow. You know, they'd really like to see more of you."

She did know. And, to a certain extent, the feeling was mutual. Yet there was the realm of memories, still too fresh, which lurked about every corner back home. She lowered her eyes defensively. "I do miss them. It's just so much more . . . comfortable . . . here. You know, I have my own life . . . no past . . ."

Mindful of the facts, he made no argument. "Are you seeing anyone special right now?"

Startled, her gaze flew to his face. For an instant, she hesitated. The whirl of emotions fogged an issue which, such a short time ago, would have been clear-cut. "No," she finally responded, willing the image of the dark and enigmatic doctor from mind.

"Look, Amber," David began, leaning across the table in earnestness, "maybe it's none of my business, but you really should go out more. You don't want to become an ornery bachelor like me, do you?"

A silken cascade slithered about her shoulders as she slowly shook her head. "Oh, no, you don't! That pitiful bachelor bit doesn't fool me for a minute. Any number of women would have been pleased to have been your wife. It's you—you've chosen the freer course. If you're ornery, you would have been even more so had you married."

"I'll never know, now, will I?" He eyed her speculatively. "But you—you're young, with a whole life ahead of you. I've never been much of a matchmaker"—he honed in on his original point—"but I happen to know a terrific guy you might enjoy . . ."

With more determination than she had felt earlier, she pressed her lips together as she shook her head. "Thanks, David, but I'm not interested right now."

He cocked his head skeptically. "Not interested in enjoying yourself? It's been three years—how long are you going to wait?"

"I have friends," she offered in self-defense. "They provide me with whatever enjoyment I need. This, tonight, is enjoyment. And I do, believe it or not, enjoy being alone at times." It was the safest way sometimes, she mused.

"Amber," his voice lowered, "you've got the whole summer to be free of all responsibility. Why not take advantage of it?"

Her tapered fingers fiddled idly with the stem of her water glass. "I am. I'm working, being lazy, following my own unstructured schedule."

"That's not what I meant, and you know it!" His more substantial hand covered hers in stress of his point. "You're not being fair to yourself, Amber. Looking back on it, you never really did have that carefree period most kids have. You and Ron were high-school sweethearts, you got married and had a child so early—hell, you've never really been involved with anyone but Ron. And the divorce has been final now for a long time. What are you waiting for?"

It was a tough question. The frown which settled over her features conveyed that much to her companion. He had hit the raw nerve. Long moments of thought passed in silence, as she tried to pinpoint the answer for herself, let alone him. "I'm not sure," she finally said, then made a stab at the crux of her feelings. "Maybe I'm just not ready for involvement yet. My life has finally begun to stabilize. I'm happy with it. Scott is. I don't want any complications just yet." The rationalization was for her own benefit; the real motivator was Zachary Wilder. This fear of involvement was the main reason it was better not to date him, given the irresistible physical draw she felt toward him.

"Involvements? Complications?" David's sharp retort brought her daydreams to an abrupt halt. "Why must there be either? All I'm talking about is companionship, fun, enjoyment, intellectual stimulation, if you will. There doesn't have to be any deeper involvement." He studied her closely, puzzled by her hesitancy.

"Okay, okay," she said with a grimace. "I know what you're thinking. You can't imagine why a woman with my age and looks doesn't have an incredibly active social life—right?" She threw him a pleading glance in accompaniment to the sing-song tone that suggested she'd heard it all before. "You can't understand why, given the number of available men around and the mores of 'young people' today, I don't just go out and have fun." She paused. When she spoke again, her voice was so soft and faraway that he nearly missed her words. "I'm just not sure that's possible . . . for me . . ."

Her brows knit as she thought once again of Zachary Wilder. Could she see him once, maybe twice, and then not again? Perhaps, she mused; but she had the uncanny conviction that a relationship with him would affect her very deeply. Whether she was ready to cope with that possibility, she just wasn't sure.

Sensing that he had lost his dinner companion to a deeper personal dilemma than she was ready to discuss with him, David shifted the topic of conversation to safer ground. "I'll be seeing your parents at the Newport races. Why don't you join us?"

The wine steward presented him with the bottle of Chablis he'd chosen, then proceeded to open it. The two at the table waited until they were once more alone, now nursing their drinks. "I don't know, David. It's difficult, sometimes. Mother and Dad try so hard. They would have me fixed up for the weekend with every eligible bachelor from

Bar Harbor to Washington. Their intentions are good, but . . ."

"Jack and Stewart will be there," he coaxed her with a lure she had to struggle to deny. Seven years her junior, the twins were her only siblings. Not only did they adore her, but they had managed to adopt Scott as their very own. But Scott was on the West Coast with his father . . .

"Naw," she wrinkled up her nose with feigned nonchalance, "if they're along, our parents will be kept busy keeping an eye on them. And anyway, the only thing Jack and Stewart see in me is Scott," she joked, tongue-in-cheek.

David's pointed gaze made his argument, complemented only by a wry "I'll bet," before he changed the subject in defeat. Amber grinned at her victory. *She* had no intention of letting her parents fill her time with unbidden courtship. Perhaps she was, despite the maturity that the years had brought, as headstrong as ever. She would make her own decisions. A momentary vision of Zachary Wilder filled her imagination, until she wished it away with a sip of wine and a taste of the lobster bisque, hot, superbly blended, and newly presented before her.

Once the matter was set aside, Amber relaxed and did enjoy herself. Her filet mignon was cooked to a perfect medium-rare, and, with the addition of lyonnaise potatoes and a salad of hearts of palm, she was suitably stuffed by the time it came to coffee. With delight, she watched David savor a piece of fresh peach pie à la mode, chatting comfortably all the while about one topic or another. It was only when they stood to leave that he broached that other subject a final time. "Now, remember, Amber," he said, offering her his arm as they walked outside toward where she had parked her car, "if you change your mind, let me know. This client of mind—a wonderful fellow— would be able to show you a very nice time. He knows all the ins and outs of Boston, and could well use your companionship as much as you could use his. Just for fun, mind you . . ."

Amber kissed him lightly on the cheek. "Thanks so much for a lovely dinner, David. And . . . I will remember . . ."

As she left the inner core of Boston and headed for her suburban retreat, his words rang repeatedly in her ears. *Just for fun*—perhaps he was right. Perhaps she did deserve to do something *just for fun*. She had had to grow up so quickly. Was she being selfish, now, to wonder about those more frivolous things she had missed? Having been repressed for so long, these thoughts were all new to her. New, and exciting, and, yes, frightening . . .

CHAPTER FOUR

Later, she was to wonder exactly how it had happened. At the time, she was tired, having been up late into the night pondering her discussion with David Brigham. She was hot, her car's airconditioner having chosen the warmest Saturday of the year, with numerous morning errands to be done, to go on the blink. And she was lonely, having just received a long and detailed letter from Scott about all of the "super" things he was doing.

It was noontime, yet she wasn't hungry. A good long cry gave her little relief from the strange tension that nagged at her insides. A lukewarm shower was, likewise, a mere stopgap measure. When her front doorbell rang, she answered it indifferently.

The sight of Zachary Wilder on her doorstep was a shot of adrenaline whose effect was instant and internal. Dark, compelling, and dressed for biking, his warm smile greeted her, then quickly cooled as he studied her pallor. There were no "Hi, how are yous?" or "Are you all rights?" Rather, he unceremoniously took her arm and drew her outside.

"You're coming with me," he growled softly. "Where's your bicycle?" Amber's senses reeled at his sudden appearance, precluding resistance. Pointing toward the garage, she stood as he raised the garage door, searched the darkness for her cycle, walked it out to her, then retrieved his own. "Here." He held a helmet, which dangled from his handlebars, out to her, then had second thoughts and fastened it securely on her head himself.

Through it all, Amber was aware only of her gratitude that he gave her no choice. It was so much easier this way; he seemed to have taken the responsibility of her well-being onto his shoulders. For the first time in as long as she could remember, she gladly yielded the burden.

Few words were spoken, other than the perfunctory "All set?" when they started off. Zachary led the way, setting a pace which, though slower than his usual, would purposely be a challenging one for Amber. Charged with nervous energy, she kept up the pace respectably. In and out of the streets of Dover they moved, dodging the occasional Saturday afternoon traffic, seeking out less-traveled roads for that reason. In the heat, her jersey grew damp. Sweat mingled with the loose strands of hair by her face, then trickled down her neck. The need to release tension drove her on, firing her legs into continual motion. Periodically, Zachary looked over his shoulder at her, smiled a smile of encouragement, then pedaled on. With gradual fatigue came the relaxation she sought. They had been pushing hard for thirty minutes when he slowed, then stopped at the side of the road, below which the river dammed and fell amid luxuriant summer growth. Graceful willows canopied the rich green-carpeted embankment. In the shade, they rested their bikes, then themselves, stretching out on the ground not far from one another.

"That was great!" she exclaimed, breathing heavily from the exertion.

His voice came from very near her ear, only slightly winded and very soothing. "I didn't work you too hard, did I?" Having rolled over onto his side from his back, he was propped up on an elbow, studying her flushed face, noting with satisfaction how completely the tension had disappeared.

She opened one lime-tinted eye to gaze up at him. Be-

67

neath his gaze, breathing became difficult once more. For a brief instant, she felt herself to be, above all else, a woman, passionate and eager to know more of the handsome man so close by her side. He was that cyclist, primitive and earthy, with his own hair damp and beads of sweat clinging to his forehead. Her finger itched to touch its moisture; clenching her fist, she restrained herself. By dint of sheer willpower, her smile was bright and mischievous.

"I did manage to keep up with you, didn't I?"

"That you did, lady," he said, grinning back admiringly.

"I'm not sure I'll be able to make it back, though. My legs are killing me!" She blushed, shaking her head. "And I thought I was getting back into shape . . ."

"Turn over."

"What?"

"Turn over." Without further ado, he flipped her over onto her stomach on the grass. "This is my specialty!" he reminded her, as his hands began an expert massage of those muscles of her legs that cried out so furiously. His long fingers kneaded every tendon, willing new life back to replace exhaustion.

Amber found herself overcome by a delightful sense of comfort, totally surrendering her limbs to his knowing hands, which moved from ankle to thigh in masterful caresses. When they jumped to commence work on the muscles of her back, she sighed her pleasure. Resistance was out of the question. She was at his mercy, a soft and pliant piece of clay in the hands of the master sculptor. His fingers molded her body, guiding it with such expertise that she prayed he would never stop. Eyes closed, she gloried in the delight he offered, oblivious to a very subtle change until his thumbs traced her spine, allowing his fingertips to skim her sides, from waist to breast and back. Her gasp was of a very different type this time. Her eyes flew open, her mind acutely aware of the nature of the feelings that his hands had aroused. When those same hands clasped her rib cage and gently turned her over, she was imprisoned in a blueness that seared its laser path into her soul. He was so close, so tender, so very, very appealing . . .

She was the woman, renewed reborn. As he had revived her muscles, so he reawakened her femininity. With awesome speed, the thrust of long-dormant yearnings filled her body, setting it apart from the very reserved woman she'd been for the past four years. This new Amber craved the feel of his lips against hers, and likewise his body. Even as that other Amber tried to resist, the battle was lost.

Her heart pounded in her throat when his hand slowly encircled it, caressing lightly, his thumb tracing the gentle curve of her soft-parted lips. A quiver of excitement coursed through her veins as she waited, waited for him to lower his mouth slowly and nibble lazily at corners of hers. It was a sure route to madness that he led her on, tantalizing her with feather-light touches until she could stand no more. For all the imaginings that he had inspired, the moment was at hand. Overwhelmed by the strength of her own need, she threaded her fingers through the damp hair by his ears, pulling his head down until the kiss was complete. At her signal, he deepened it, parting her lips further with his own, gently caressing them, coaxing the response which had been so long denied yet waited, just below the surface, for expression.

Amber was drawn instantly into the vortex of his passion, returning his kiss with every bit of the feeling he generated in her. His tongue forayed into the depths of her mouth, startling her with its aggression, until her own first sampled, then tasted his in turn, to her utter rapture. When he drew back to look down at her once more, his eyes mirrored her mounting passion.

Amber was drugged into euphoria by the maleness of him. Helplessly, she returned his gaze expectantly, invitingly. Her hands fell to his shoulders, where they lay in appreciation of the firm-corded muscles beneath the molded fabric of his jersey. If she had once possessed restraint, it was now a far memory. For Zachary brought out the woman in her—blind in passion, naked in desire. For the short moment, she indulged herself. It had been so long since she had recognized the physical cravings of her body, that her trembling thrill was akin to that of a virgin, being awakened for the first time.

Zachary's hands were balanced on the grass on either side of her shoulders, his body slanted over hers in gentle possession. Awareness of the world about dissipated beneath the soul-touch of his gaze. What she felt, at that moment, was too lovely either to analyze or to disturb.

"It's been a long time for you, hasn't it?" he asked, his finger running the curve of her cheek, then coming to rest at the pulse point of her neck. With the acceleration of her heartbeat, he had his answer. Her brilliant green gaze held his as she nodded shyly. The facts were there, but he couldn't understand them. "Why, Amber? You're a beautiful woman. Why have you held that passion of yours under such a tight lock and key?" His hand slid to her shoulder, then traced a provocative path between her breasts, tormenting yet elusive, before stilling in claim of her midriff.

Threatened by the intensity of his questioning, she lightly scoffed it off. "Would you have me sleeping around, Dr. Wilder?"

The tightening of his jaw indicated his opinion of her humor. "That's not what I meant, and you know it. There's promiscuity, and then there's . . . passion. One is cheap, the other very beautiful."

"With a very fine line between the two," she interjected, growing more serious in response. Were the two, indeed, separable? What she felt now, lying on the ground, partly beneath Zachary's heady maleness, was vivid passion. Yet she barely knew him, if the truth be told. That the physical attraction between them was powerful, breathtaking—she

70

did not doubt. But could she give herself totally to him—and call it passion? Or, given the privacy of a bedroom and the irresponsibility of her summer's life-style, would that passion be synonymous with promiscuity? She had loved Ron—then had slept with him. Could the physical fulfillment come first? The question, asked in the far recesses of her mind, brought a flicker of doubt to her otherwise soft expression. Suddenly unsure of herself, she squirreled from beneath him, stood up, and retrieved her helmet, her back to him all the while.

The whisper of the wind in the willow overhead blended with the whisper in her ear moments later. "I won't give up that easily, Amber." Strong brown arms circled her waist from behind, drawing her back to fit snugly against his body. "We have so much in common, so much to offer each other. You may fight it, but you'd be doomed to failure. Why not face it now? Haven't you ever felt that something was inevitable?"

Her breath caught in her throat at the feel of his sinewy thighs against hers. Yet reason lurked in the breeze. "Yes," she murmured softly, "I've felt that." It took little effort to shift around in his arms to face him, much more to look into his eyes. "I felt it that day at the airport, that day I saw you at the Wellesley campus, and again that day in your office. But," her voice was harsher, rent now with pain, "I also felt it the day Ron and I decided to get married. And look at the heartache *that's* caused."

For long moments, he said nothing. Their eyes locked in silent conversation, each reliving the agony of his own past, as though to exorcise it from the present. But it wasn't as easily done, for the past was with each of them in the form of the child conceived in that past, a child who meant the world to that respective parent. Pulled in many directions at once, Amber's gaze blurred. As tears trickled down her cheeks, he pulled her to him, cradling her head against his broad chest, rubbing her neck and back soothingly. Once again, his nearness lulled her to forgetfulness.

71

Her nostrils breathed in his scent, her hands reveled in the strength of the rippling muscles of his back, to which she clung. When she finally lifted her face, he kissed the path of her tears with the understanding she had counted on. His ministrations culminated at her lips in a kiss that was gentle and sweet, firm yet patient, and full of promise. Snapping her helmet by her ear once more, he touched her lips a final time, adjusted his own headgear, and mounted his bicycle. She followed suit.

"Ach . . ." she moaned spontaneously, flipping from grimace to laugh in an instant, appalled at the soreness of her backside when she so nonchalantly resumed the saddle. "I think . . . you . . . missed a spot!" She giggled softly. Her blush of embarrassment gave her all the more a look of vulnerability, arousing within him a fierce protectiveness.

His voice was husky, his smile teased her gallantly. "I'll have a look at it when we get back—they're apt to arrest us here." His deep blue eyes scanned the embankment, noting the few other people dotting its expanse. When he turned back to her, his amusement was open. "Think you can make it, old lady?"

With a defiant chuckle, she eagerly nibbled his bait. "If you can, so can I!" After all, he was, according to the résumé she had devoured ravenously at the office, a full ten years older than she. Moments later, she was to have grave doubts as to the wisdom of her eagerness. Bolstered by pride, however, the soreness soon passed into numbness, enabling her to follow on the tail of the white-backed biker before her, feeling much like the greyhound following the rabbit at the racetrack. The invigoration of the ride had cleared out the cobwebs in her mind, enough to relegate her stiffness to the ranks of the unimportant. The good doctor thought differently, and though he made no move to reinforce his skill as a masseur, he delivered his order without hesitancy.

"Why don't you go in and take a long soak. I'll pick you

up in an hour. Sound all right?" The intimacy of his gaze thrilled her, stiffness and all.

"An hour? Where are we going?" Was this the date she had put off for so long? she asked herself. No, she reasoned good-naturedly, the bike ride had been the date; this was merely a bonus. And, having gotten that "first date" out of the way, she continued in silent but light-headed humor, she would relax and enjoy herself.

Holding the door for him to follow her into the house, she headed for the pitcher of iced tea in the refrigerator, pouring two tall ice-filled glasses of the light brown liquid. He accepted his gratefully, draining it with a haste that would make any internist cringe, then answered her. "There's a good French film playing at the Nickelodeon. We could catch the early show, then drive over to Harvard Square for dinner. There's always something going on on a Saturday night."

Amber nodded her delight. *"Oui, monsieur! Comme je sais bien!"*

"Ohhhh, no." His eyes narrowed in mock anger. "Are you one of those who don't have to watch the subtitles? If so, forget it—I refuse to see a foreign film with a linguist! I tried that once; she spent the entire flick telling me everything *else* that was being said, that the subtitles left out."

An enchanted ripple of laughter erupted through her smile. "Heavens, no! You've just heard my full vocabulary. I've forgotten everything else! But, actually," she teased, growing more excited as she spoke, "you don't have to read the subtitles in those French works to get the gist of the film. It's all in the tone." Hers had lowered to mime the seductive quality to which she referred, drawing out the last words deliciously.

Zachary's appreciative grin flashed reward enough for her attempt at drama. With a devilish wink of the eye, he was off, leaving her alone to ponder, despite her clamoring muscles, her growing state of relaxation. There was a naturalness about him—about them, together—which she could not deny, a rightness that was pure instinct. Perhaps it was simply wishful thinking—but she fully intended to indulge in the fantasy, for the evening, at least!

An hour later, he entered her living room through the front door she always left unlocked. It was a questionable habit, though one that was particularly practical with a child going in and out all day. His frown suggested that he thought she might be more careful, now that she was alone.

"Amber? . . . Amber?" he called, walking to the bottom of the stairway.

Her voice came muted from a distant bedroom. "I'll be right down, Zachary. Would you believe . . . I fell asleep in the tub. You wore me out!" Having finished applying a light coat of makeup, she pulled the thick blond mane off her neck and twisted it for pinning.

"Leave it down. It looks pretty that way." The mirror's reflection showed Zachary standing directly behind her. Stunned by his sudden appearance in her bedroom, she looked down quickly.

"You should have waited downstairs. What if I wasn't dressed?"

"So much the better." His head dipped to give his lips access to the back of her still-exposed neck, then he took a step back, allowing her to let her hair fall. Disturbed viscerally by his presence, her hand shook as she brushed the long blond tresses into a semblance of order, then stood for his inspection. She got more than she expected, his eyes lingering hungrily on the curve of her hips and the swell of her breasts, both outlined softly by the lightweight sundress she wore.

"Perfect!" he complimented her, his lips twitching up at her momentary shyness, then thinning as quickly. "I should have stayed here, though. Do you have any idea what could happen if you fall asleep in the bath?"

Amber smiled meekly. "The water was shallow."

"If the water was shallow, how could it have helped those sore muscles? And besides"—his sternness melted as quickly as it had materialized—"I might have been able to scrub your back."

Trying her best to downplay the blatant sensuality of his words, she turned to fetch a small white shoulder bag to blend with the dress. "I really do feel much better now," she murmured quietly, vibrantly aware of his tall form close behind.

Once at the bottom of the stairs, he disappeared into the kitchen, returning a moment later with a more satisfied gleam in his eye. "Have you got your key?" She stared in puzzlement, as he proceeded to turn the lock of the front door also, making his point clear. Amber was not about to argue.

"It's right over there," she gestured to the hall table. "Would you like to hold it for me, to make sure I don't lose it?" Her sweetness was edged by the quiver of lips which threatened to erupt into laughter.

Deep blue eyes pierced her instantly. "Don't get smart with me, Amber." His warning was in all seriousness, its force as unfathomable to her as its cause.

"I was only kidding," she whispered lightly, relieved to see the gradual softening of his face. "Shouldn't we be going?"

The air-cooled interior of the silver BMW was a welcome respite from the summer's heat. As they sped toward Boston, Amber dared to study the man in the driver's seat. Wearing crisp white ducks and a navy shirt, rolled to the elbow and unbuttoned to a rakish point below the throat, his appearance stirred her senses with maddening force. He was cleanly shaven, his hair neatly combed. The forearms that extended to the steering wheel were tanned and finely matted with the same vibrant dark hair that lined the open vee of his shirt. The intimate confines of the car seemed under his total command, as was the rest of the world he touched. By the time they reached the theater, she welcomed the relief of a larger, more open, less suggestive space.

Her relief was short-lived. The film was the most soft and seductive piece of artwork she had ever seen on the screen. Had she realized it would be so, she might never have agreed to see it with Zachary. Understated and magnificently photographed, as was so much French work, it was both romantic and alluring. The sound track carried a poignancy which the dialogue of whispers augmented. It was a love story, powerfully done, exquisitely tender.

More than once, her pulse raced in time with the heroine's, though her hero was seated beside her, watching as was she. More than once, she gripped her hands together in her lap, lest she reach for his. More than once, she ached for the arm that might have gone about her shoulder and brought her head against his chest, yet he remained engrossed in the picture. As the climax of the movie neared, her pink-glossed lip bore the brunt of her frustration, even white teeth digging mercilessly into it, as she rued the unfairness of the situation. *It was a conspiracy,* she concluded sourly, bent on driving her into the arms of Zachary Wilder. He must have planned this; perhaps he had even brought other dates to this very same movie. *It simply wasn't fair!*

"Well, madame, what did you think?" The broad grin which dazzled her as they exited the theater melted any of her testiness. The problem was her own overfantasizing subconscious. Was she love-starved, or, more specifically, sex-starved? Perhaps she *should* have begun to date sooner. Then her present frustration might have been put into perspective.

"It was an excellent film! Very well done!" The understatement of her rating brought a devilish twist to the male lips that now lowered to nestle in her hair, breathing softly against it.

"Not very helpful for the peace of mind, though, was it?"

The flush that crept up her neck was observed before she could will it into abeyance. That strong arm was about her shoulders now, holding her to his hip as they walked to the car. As though facing a combustible situation, the two were silent during the ten-minute ride across the river to Cambridge and into Harvard Square. An electrical current circulated between them, charging the air with its force. It was only after they had parked and left the car to begin a stroll around the Square that Amber felt herself relax once more.

Harvard Square was a treat she had indulged in soon after she'd arrived in the Boston area. Though Cambridge was an entity in and of itself, Harvard Square was its hub. The atmosphere here was academic and intellectual, with bookstores dominating the window fronts and students populating the walks. Diversity was the password, high color the rule. The flavor of the Square shifted from season to season, as did its population. Now, in summertime, the air was warm and humid, yet strangely light and free. It was a time of summer sessions, of less concentrated study, of indulgent gaiety. The streets were given up wholly to evening adventurers, many of whom had come to sample the unique spice of the Square—as had Amber and Zach.

Her hand lay lightly in his as they walked, working their way slowly through the leisurely crowd, stopping on one corner to hear an impromptu jazz concert, on another to appreciate a similarly staged folk group. "They didn't have these in my day," he mused by her ear. "Things seemed so much more studious then. You know, everyone scurrying around the Square loaded with books . . ." His gaze was faraway, in another time. "We used to study late, then head over for an Elsie's Special." Remembering her presence, he looked warmly down at her. "You don't know what an Elsie's Special is, do you?" Amber shook her head, wondering more critically who the "we" of his adventure was. "An Elsie's Special was a roast beef sandwich on a bulkie roll, with huge piles of meat, thin slices of onion, and a healthy portion of Russian dressing—all for seventy-five cents." He shook his head. "That was a long time ago." Again, the distant glaze of his eyes took him from her, albeit for a brief moment. At the instant that she would have asked if he'd known his wife here, he laughed more lightly. "You must be starved. Let's go get something to eat. There is a terrific little French restaurant right around the corner; it will go well with the movie." The playful nip he gave her middle brought out her own laugh, setting the tone of their dinner.

For nearly two hours, Amber put aside every fear, every worry, every inhibition. Sitting across the small corner table from one another, they exchanged tales of various happy times in their lives, many of the more recent vintage that excluded mention of their prospective former spouses. Zachary filled her in on a recent conference he attended, comprised of leg men, back men, arm men, joint men, nose men, and the occasional female orthopedist. To Amber's gay laughter at the categorization of his colleagues, he added, "There was one fellow who specialized in fingers—Dr. Knuckleman." She snickered skeptically. "No, I'm serious," he assured her, barely stifling his own guffaw. "At least, I'm not one of the gastroenterologists. The thought of belonging to a 'gas group' or going to a 'liver meeting' never much appealed to me."

When their mutual laughter subsided, she went on to tell him of the various free-lance pieces she'd done, including a memorable one of a car wash. "You know, the type where you sit in your car and watch the long gray fingers slither up and over your windshield," which had given her nightmares for weeks afterward. "I created a verbal monster in that piece—it came back to haunt me. I've never been one for horror flicks."

Much later, when they returned to Dover, Amber invited him in for a nightcap. "Ah, you'd better make that coffee," she apologized, as soon as the invitation had left her lips. "I don't keep a supply of liquor around the house."

His eyes warmed her as much as a drink might have. "That will be fine."

Mugs in hands, she led him through the kitchen to the back porch, an open veranda with a long wooden bench-type swing. A gentle breeze had begun to stir, bringing with it the only hope of coolness that the night would offer. Aside from the chorus of crickets, all was still and peaceful. The swing rocked gently beneath their joint weight.

"Tell me about your marriage," he suggested softly. The faint light of the kitchen cast a golden glow to his profile, yet she didn't need it to tell her that his eyes were on her.

Her marriage and its failure were the last thing that she wanted to discuss, the last thing that she expected Zachary to want to hear about. "You don't really want to listen to that melodrama, do you?" she chided doubtfully.

His answer was blunt. "Yes."

There were few people with whom she had discussed her past. That she should even consider doing it now, with Zachary Wilder, a relatively new acquaintance, bemused her. Yet, from the very first, she had sensed the understanding he had of her experiences, as though his had been very similar. It seemed perfectly normal that she should tell him everything.

"Ron and I were childhood friends, then sweethearts," she began, staring off into the darkness as her mind traveled back in years. "We came from the same town; our parents were friends. We went to school together, right through high school. When his family moved from Maryland to the West Coast, it was understandable that we should both apply to schools there. By some *miracle*"— she emphasized the word, wondering what the future would have held had that "miracle" not occurred—"we were both accepted to Stanford. We were young and very

79

idealistic. Despite our parents' objections, we eloped the summer before our freshman year." Her blond head turned toward Zachary as she sought to justify her actions. He sat quietly, listening closely, watching intently. Strangely intimidated, she lapsed into silence.

"Go on," he urged softly.

Breathing deeply, she looked down at her coffee mug. In hindsight, she had been so foolish, so shortsighted. "It seemed to make sense at the time. You know, economical. Less expensive for us to live together than apart, type of thing."

"Why didn't you just *live* together?" When Zachary had been an undergraduate, one didn't "live with" someone. The sexual revolution came about while he was in medical school, but he had been too busy to pay it much heed. And, anyway, he had already met Sheila.

"I was raised in a very strict home. It was bad enough that we eloped, depriving my parents of their only daughter's big extravaganza of a wedding. Had we decided to live together without benefit of marriage, I would have been disowned." But to blame her parents, totally, was unfair. "And it was me, too. I would have felt . . . uncomfortable . . ." That she felt old-fashioned was absurd, considering the status of sexual mores today. But she would have made the same decision over again. "As it turned out, it was a lucky thing that we did marry. I was pregnant within three months." A sad laugh slipped through her lips. "We were so naive. Everything was bound to go our way. I never even bothered with birth control!"

"You must have wanted a baby."

Stunned, her glance flew through the darkness to the depth of his blue eyes. Considering the situation from the more objective perch on which she now sat, a baby was the last thing the two of them had needed at the tender age of nineteen. Once again, Zachary had weeded through the superfluous thought to get right to the nitty-gritty. "Yes,

I suppose I did. At least, once I knew I was pregnant, I was excited. It was . . . another thing . . . that the young and all-powerful could do." Sarcasm etched the truth of her feelings at the time.

"What about college?" he prompted her gently.

The lilt of her tone held self-ridicule. "Oh, that was no problem. I mean, with our parents to support us—which they did, despite their opposition to our marriage—we could hire people to watch Scottie while we were at class. It was actually very easy to arrange . . ." Her voice trailed off; Scottie *had* been the least of her worries from that point on.

As though following her thought, Zachary jumped to the punch line. "What happened?"

This was the hardest part to face. Deep within her remained a lingering taste of humiliation, of hurt, of bitterness, of shock. For long moments, the serenity of the night served to soothe her, giving her, finally, the courage to explain. "Neither of us had ever dated anyone else. I never felt the need; Ron did. After Scott was born, when I was more limited in movement, Ron began to feel his oats. I suppose it was only natural that he should wonder about what he missed. He had made many friends at Stanford—we both had. But his were more aggressive." She sighed. "To make a long story short, he spread his wings and took flight. Oh, he came back to us every few days or so, but we never . . . slept . . . together after that." The hand that nonchalantly lifted the weight of her hair off her neck and gave access to the night air trembled slightly. The sense of inadequacy which that disastrous marriage had bequeathed her was all too vivid for her. If there was one thing that had haunted her over the years, it was that she had somehow been lacking, that her husband had sought refuge elsewhere when she had been unable to give him what he needed.

Head hung low, the curtain of her hair shielded her face from Zachary's. When his strong fingers cupped her chin

81

to turn her toward him, she flinched. Persistently, he wound his hands through her hair, forcing her head around. When she kept her eyes downcast, he reproved her softly. "Look at me, Amber." Reluctantly, she lifted her gaze to meet his. "Don't blame yourself," he urged, reading her thoughts as though they had all been spoken aloud. "That happens with men—with women, too. The need to explore, to experiment, sexually, if in no other way, is a common phenomenon."

"But *I* never wanted to—" she began, the hurt pouring from her gaze.

"That's the kind of person *you* are, Amber. Not everyone is like you are. Your husband was different. He must have felt the need, at that stage in his life, to satisfy a curiosity—"

"Did you?" The words slipped out unintentionally, but she wouldn't take them back, even given the chance.

His hands fell to her shoulders, then back to the small wooden rail between them. "Yes, I did. I had my heyday, way back there." His admission contained neither pride nor bravado; as he offered it, it was a statement of fact. "I didn't settle down until I was a med student, with that wanderlust behind me."

"And how would *you* have felt if your wife suddenly decided that you weren't enough of a man for her?" she blurted impulsively.

"She did." His words hit her like dead weight, clearing her head of self-pity instantly.

"W-what?" It seemed impossible.

His eyes held hers steadily as he elaborated. "My wife took up with my best friend after six years of marriage and with a young child at home." If he felt anger and bitterness, it was well hidden.

"How could she?" she cried out in astonishment.

Zachary laughed broadly, incongruously delighted at her response. "Very easily. I was on duty when my friend was off. She had the best of both worlds. I just happened

82

to come home unexpectedly one day to find them in bed together."

"How horrible!" At least Ron had held his tête-à-têtes far from their apartment. The devastation would have been that much worse if he had thumbed his nose at her as blatantly as Zachary's wife had done to him.

His tone had sobered. "It was . . . at the time. Very ugly. I understand that she's been through quite a few other men since. I only hope," he clenched his jaw, "that she has enough sense to be discreet about her social life while Liz is with her."

Now she sensed his frustration, yet words of comfort eluded her. Rather, she leaned tentatively toward him, winding her arms around his waist and daring to rest her head against the solid wall of his chest. Driven by the need to somehow assuage the loneliness that he must have felt —that she had felt herself—she offered him her warmth in silence. Slowly, his arms moved to close the circle, tightening imperceptibly at her sigh.

They remained locked together for long moments of comfort from the hurts of the past. If Amber had initiated the gesture, his steel-banded hold returned it in full. Her ear rested flush against his heart, its steady beat a lulling song. This was the closeness she had craved all evening, though its innocence decried all suggestiveness. She felt strangely happy and complete in Zachary's arms, and she gave herself up to the strength of his sanctuary. Here she was safe from the world. Within his protection, nothing could harm her.

Then, slowly, his hands began a gentle massage of her back, sketching small circles on the soft fabric of her sundress. When the beat of his heart grew less even, her own kept pace. A tingle of excitement radiated from his fingertips, traveling the length of her and back. It was the birth of a feeling she could not deny, the same burgeoning awareness of her needs and longings, woman to his man, that she'd discovered that afternoon. Although a small voice within cried for caution, the bulk of her senses surged forward. She held herself back from him for a brief moment, disturbing his play. Even in the darkness, his eyes mirrored the very pleasure she felt. It was too much to resist, this need to be purely selfish, to grasp at the stars. Happily, she let her head fall back to his chest. He was so strong and confident, she mused—and he made her feel so very, very feminine.

When his hand moved up to caress her shoulder, she answered in kind, allowing her fingers the freedom to inch toward the open neck of his shirt, there reveling in the fine tufts of hair, thrilling at the warmth that seeped from him. A heat began its molten circulation in her veins, totally aside from the summer's heat, dissipated now under the newly emergent moon. His fingers teased her, circling the curve of her shoulder, then falling lower to tempt the gentle swell of her breast at the bodice of her dress. The thin spaghetti strap was all that kept his hand from her skin; as he toyed around it, she grew fuller in anticipation.

With a soft moan, she tilted her head upward. "Do you have any idea—" Her hoarse whisper was swallowed by his mouth as it seized her lips with the hunger she felt herself. When he finally relented and cupped the fullness of her breast to his palm, a quiver shook her. With it came a trace of reason. "Zachary—?" she asked, pleaded against his neck, knowing all too well what she wanted from this man, yet still fearful of taking it.

"Shhhh, Amber. It feels good, doesn't it?" The huskiness of his voice betrayed his own emotional state.

"Yes, but—"

"Then let me. You deserve this. There's no harm in being selfish for a change, is there?" At that moment, as his words echoed her own earlier thoughts, she yielded to them willingly. He seemed to have a way with both her mind and her body. And he gave her nothing but pleasure.

Sighing her agreement, she wound both arms about the tanned column of his neck, gasping when he slipped a hand beneath her knees and swung her into his arms. "Where are you taking me?" she shrieked, oddly amused.

The wicked gleam in his eye burst forth as they left the cover of the porch and he descended the few steps to the grassy yard. "Soft grass and dim moonlight are a hell of a lot more comfortable than a hard wooden swing and the shadows. I want to see you."

He eased her gently down on her back atop the lawn, then stretched his length beside her, his body leaning half over hers. With her arms maintaining a neck hold, she looked up at him, startled by the near reverence she saw in his eyes, moments before so full of mischief. The similar expression on her own face was blotted out when his head lowered to resume his kiss, this time with a tenderness that cried out to her very depths. Instinctively, she arched toward him, rewarded when his hand circled her breast again, caressing and teasing, skimming its taut peak, then retreating to an exploration of the lines of her hip. All past receded; there was only the now. Drowning in the ocean of his passion, she could not think one step further than where he took her at a given instant. When his hand slid beneath the thin strap of her dress and slipped it over her shoulder, her excitement grew. When the soft fabric was drawn down to expose the creamy softness of her breast, she held her breath. When his eyes slid from her face to that gleaming orb and his hand quickly followed suit, she moaned her delight. Her breast filled his palm, his thumb coaxed its bud to even greater firmness. When she would have cried out, his mouth swooped down to smother the sound, slanting hungrily across her lips as she trembled.

The fire of desire seared through her, fanned by the tongue that rolled over and around her nipple, causing wave after wave of sensual shock. But her need was to touch as well, to reacquaint herself with the swelling masculinity before her. She was an equal player in the drama, adapting to her role with little hesitancy.

His shirt lay suddenly open, its buttons released by her

85

hands in their bid to know him further. When he lifted her off the grass, eased off her other shoulder strap, and drew her dress down to her waist, she curved her arms around him and brought herself into his embrace, heady and warm, his chest a brand against the bareness of her breasts.

"So beautiful, Amber," he groaned, barely holding his control in check, his hands spanning her back, covering its every inch. Her breath caught in her throat as he clutched her convulsively to him. Then, he lay her down, cuffing her wrists to the ground on either side of her shoulders. His eyes devoured the silver-sheened upthrust of her breasts, delighting in her seminakedness for a long moment, before covering her body with his.

She was at once engulfed in a flood surge of emotion, crying for release from within as his ardent touch drove her to distraction. His lips rained kisses on her face, trailing a sensuous path down her neck to her throat and across her body. Against her thigh, his arousal was a vivid fact.

Burying her hands in the fullness of his dark hair, she arched closer against him. But when his hand slid beneath her dress to caress the silken smoothness of her thigh, an enigmatic and unbidden force made her stiffen. "Please, Zachary," she whimpered, "please . . ."

Ragged gasping disturbed the normal velvet flow of his words. "Please, what, honey?" He raised himself on an elbow and searched her face, its glow now from passion as well as the moon. "Please make love to you . . . or please stop?" She gasped at his question, only then realizing the extent of her abandonment. Even amid her delirium, she caught the note of urgency in his tone. "If I don't stop now, I won't be able to. I'd like nothing better than to take you, right here, beneath that moon." Long, strong fingers rested intimately on the bareness of her torso, tempting inches from the waistband of her dress and beyond. "Your body is ready for me, Amber. Are your emotions?"

The dilemma was all too real; he had summed it up precisely. As reason slowly returned, she knew that, despite the fiery cravings of her body, fully awakened after a long sleep, she was not yet ready to commit herself to the kind of relationship that entailed the totality of lovemaking. Indeed, her body had betrayed its awesome need. Yet, once fulfilled, would she fall prey to a new kind of bondage?

A new dimension of the situation chose that moment to enter her mind whirl. If she refused to yield to his possession, might she lose him? What they had shared during their time together this day was precious. She had felt more whole, in his company, than she had for so long. He made her feel like a woman, a beautiful woman, who *did* have it in her power to satisfy him. The tremor of his muscles, as he held himself suspended over her, told of his own susceptibility. Without a doubt, it was gratifying to her ego. But was it lust—or a deeper attraction to her as a person?

The doubts which raged through her features gave him the answer to his question. Without another word, he sat her up and eased her dress back until its straps hugged the hollow of her shoulders once more. Then, with a low groan, he lay back on the grass, inhaling deeply, struggling to calm his surging virility. Sensing his battle, she did not touch him, but sat several feet away and helplessly witnessed the labored rise and fall of his chest.

"You're amazing, do you know that?" she finally whispered her gratitude.

One eye opened to spear her. "And how am I amazing?" Though his tone held a lingering hoarseness, it had chilled noticeably.

"I would have let you, if you had pushed me. Why didn't you? I was pretty senseless, there, for a while." Her confession poured freely forth, bolstered by the knowledge that he hadn't, that he wouldn't, take advantage of her.

Disturbed by her words, he threw an arm across his

eyes. For a fearful moment, she wondered if he suddenly regretted not having satisfied his very obvious physical need when he'd had the chance. But when he finally spoke, his words were even, his thoughts fully rational. The arm lowered to uncover a strange harshness in his eyes.

"I don't want a senseless woman, Amber. I want a woman who knows exactly what she is doing, who wants it with both her body and her mind. You're no babe in the woods, any more than you are a virgin. By now, you should know that lovemaking is a two-sided thing. There's more to it than . . ." His words died on his lips as he withdrew his thought abruptly. Then, in one fluid movement, he sat up to face her, his shirttails streaming behind him on the grass. Leaning forward, he put a fierce hand around the back of her neck. "When we make love, it's going to be the most beautiful thing you have ever experienced in your life." His sense of conviction sent a shaft of fear through her, but his next words were strangely comforting. "And it's going to be that way for me, too. A man can find release many ways, Amber, when the physical need becomes too great. But at this stage in my life, the need is far more than the purely physical. I can wait."

To Amber's ear, his declaration was a perfect ending of a perfect day. When he kissed her a final time, it was without demand of any sort. Leading her into the house, he deposited their empty coffee mugs in the kitchen sink, then proceeded to the front door. Even then, a small part of her cried out for him to stay, to spend the night with her, to give her more of the delight he had so eloquently promised. But sanity prevailed.

"I've got to work tomorrow," he said gently. "I'm preparing a lecture for my trip to Atlanta on Monday. Why don't I talk with you when I get back?"

Her lips curved softly into a smile. "That's fine."

As he opened the front door to leave, his eyes narrowed. "You behave yourself . . . and lock this door, do you hear?"

At her nod, he turned and descended the walk to his car, driving off down the road without another look back. Amber's eyes followed the twin taillights until they were swallowed by the night. Slowly, she turned, closed the door, and locked it, as a grin spread across her face. He was gone, yet she wasn't alone. The memory of his bold presence lent a richness to her existence that precluded loneliness. The large brass bed upstairs welcomed her that night, its sheets cool and soothing against her fevered skin. Silence filled the darkness, broken only by the intermittent chirp of the crickets, the occasional howl of the basset hound down the street, beneath the oaks and maples. In her mind, Zach was beside her, holding her, caressing her, leading her to heights of ecstasy and joining her there. As the peace of the night slowly filtered through her limbs, she slept. She was in the eye of the storm, unaware that the following morning would bring a return of all the old doubts and a smattering of new ones—plus a most disturbing phone call to Scott.

CHAPTER FIVE

In the dark of night, there had been only Amber and Zachary. With daylight came the world of other things, each bearing its own mind link to reality. As the sun climbed higher, her doubts multiplied. She questioned both the prudence of her behavior the night before and, more generally, the course her feelings had run for the past week. Though the amount of time she had spent with Zachary was, in relative terms, small, she *did* feel that she knew him, and he her, better than many acquaintances of years. Yet his presence in her life took her completely by surprise; she was totally unprepared for the sort of relationship that theirs promised. Things had happened too quickly—her head reeled.

Puttering around the house this Sunday morning, finding one inconsequential chore after another to perform, she reminded herself that Zachary Wilder was only the second man she had ever really known romantically. Not only did the fact of her attraction to him startle her, but she was shocked by its strength. In her experience with Ron, things had built slowly, gradually over the years, from childhood, to adolescence, to adulthood. When sexual awareness grew, it likewise had progressed in steps.

Zachary Wilder was another matter. His overwhelming virility had taken her by storm. Granted, she was a mature, sophisticated woman now, no longer a virgin and with a preadolescent son to prove it. But her total abandonment in Zachary's arms astonished—and worried—

her. After so many years of showing, of feeling no interest in a physical relationship, why now had she suddenly rediscovered the flame of desire banked deep within her? What was it about Zachary that reduced her to a quivering mass of femininity? And what good could come of these wanton instincts? Hadn't she made the mistake, once before, of letting her heart and emotions overrule reason? Then, she had emerged from the ordeal with a beautiful, healthy child whom she adored, and a heart full of pain and disillusionment. Could she risk the same now? It was untenable to contemplate such lunacy. Yet, how easily things might have gotten out of hand, had not Zachary, himself, offered a wedge of sanity.

Self-directed fury engulfed her. How very naive she continued to be, relying on a man to make things right! In hindsight, she saw that she had, perhaps, been the stronger partner in her relationship with Ron. Could she assume differently, in any future relationship with Zachary? But was she being fair to him, expecting him to take the responsibility for caution in a heady sexual encounter? He was a man, with normal physical needs—and he had denied those needs, once, for her benefit. Would he do it again? Could she *ask* him to do it again? Another man would have taken advantage of her the first time. Zachary hadn't. Why not? Despite the explanation he had offered, her long-held skepticism prevailed.

The answer to the question eluded her, though one other thing was clear: she simply could not expect him to be her conscience again. It was *her* responsibility; she would have to answer to her own actions. If making love with Zachary was what she wanted to do, she might indulge in the heavy petting of the night past. On the other hand, if she was not prepared to surrender in full to him, she had no business leading him on.

In the wake of this soul-searching, as the pretense of doing chores gave way to an aimless pacing of the floor, she made two vows. In the first place, she would *not* allow herself the state of abandonment she had experienced last night *until* the time came that she was willing to see it through. It was both compromising to her own self-respect and unfair to Zachary.

In the second place, she would begin to date more. Perhaps it was the effect of the long starvation diet she'd been on which had enhanced the manly offerings of Zachary Wilder. If so, the only solution was to broaden her exposure. Corey might help her in that bid, as might David Brigham, both of whom had offered so recently. The summer, with Scott away, was a perfect opportunity —as both of her friends had bluntly pointed out to her. Resolve was strong to take them up on their gallant offers.

These tentative decisions having been made, Amber put through her regular call to Scott. When a strange female voice, disturbingly groggy sounding at what would have been nine thirty in the morning, West Coast time, answered the phone, an odd disquietude fell over her. Scott, however, coming on the line within the minute, was as ebullient as ever.

"Hey, Mom," he burst out, fast on the heels of the customary "hi's" and "how are you's," "you'll never guess what! Dad is getting married again."

Stunned and speechless for a moment, Amber struggled to integrate this information. The passage of time had served to remove any lingering feelings she harbored toward Ron even after that initial anger and hurt had destroyed most of them. There were no thoughts of reconciliation, nor had there ever been, since that day she had finally decided on a divorce. But the news that Scott was to have a stepmother shook her. For some unfathomable reason, she suddenly felt threatened . . . and more alone than ever.

"That's very nice, Scottie," she finally managed to offer. His excitement was obvious and innocent. For years she had made the supreme effort never to taint Ron in Scott's mind. Now, she wrestled with her own feelings to keep from squelching the young boy's enthusiasm. "Do you like her?"

"Sure, Mom! She's really nice." The image of the wide-opened eyes in the sandy-haired head of her son brought moistness to her eyes. She missed him. But he sounded very content. "Her name is Marietta and she has blond hair like yours and she's really pretty. They're getting married in two weeks, so I'll be able to be in the wedding." The knot in Amber's stomach tightened again.

The slight tremor of her voice was absorbed by the long-distance telephone lines. "That's very exciting. Your father must be pleased." She chewed her lip, praying that her words did not have the bitter overtone in Scott's hearing that they had in hers.

Mercifully, the boy was oblivious. "He is, Mom. And, guess what?"

"What?"

"They're going away by themselves for a few days after the wedding," he began, "but then they're coming back to pick me up. We're all going to the Grand Canyon." It was one of the Seven Wonders of the World; Scott's voice conveyed the appropriate relish.

"Oh, hon, that's terrific! You'll love the Grand Canyon!" In her heart, Amber knew he would—and she was grateful to her ex-husband for wanting to take him, new wife and all. "How long will you be there?"

The conversation went on for another ten minutes, proceeding to a run-down of the other things that filled Scott's California days, aside from the impending marriage. Amber hung up the phone thoroughly convinced that her son was healthy and happy—but inexplicably distraught herself. On impulse, she lifted the receiver again. Within two hours, she was firmly ensconced in a corner of the white wicker love seat at the apartment of her friend, Corey, in Brookline.

"Okay, love, tell Mother what's bothering you," the

redheaded woman demanded gently, plopping her slender form on the opposite end of the love seat.

Speaking her own thoughts aloud, Amber began. "It really bothers me that he's getting married again, and I can't, for the life of me, imagine why!" The shimmering olive gaze that settled on her friend reflected her confusion.

"Well, then, let's take it step by step," the other suggested, her analytical approach to life and medicine coming to the fore. "Do you miss Ron?"

"No!"

"Are you sorry you got the divorce?"

"No!"

"Good." A broad smile creased her friend's soft complexion. "Now that we have *that* out of the way, let's get down to brass tacks. Scott sounded pleased with the situation?"

A mild frown passed over Amber's forehead. "Yes."

"And that bothers you?"

After a long pause and with great self-disdain, Amber grimaced. "In a way, yes."

"Go on," Corey prodded, seeking those emotions in Amber which she, herself, would have felt in the circumstances.

Amber hesitated, struggling to find the words to express her jumbled feelings. "I want Scottie to be happy, and he *did* seem to be, on the phone. But . . . there is that tiny voice in me that wants . . . Scott . . . to hate . . . that woman."

Corey's sensitivity precluded any mockery. "Jealousy."

"Of her as Ron's wife, *no!* Of her as Scott's stepmother" —her voice lowered in reluctant confession—"yes."

"But that's perfectly natural, Amber. You've been the only mother Scott has known; the thought of his having a stepmother is bound to be a threat."

Grateful that her friend understood, Amber smiled

sadly. "I suppose it was inevitable that it would happen one day. But that doesn't make it any easier to accept."

"I know, love. I know." Corey leaned forward and lightly patted her friend's knee. "You just have to get used to the idea. And there is really nothing for you to feel threatened by. After all, by court order, you have Scott for ten months out of every year."

"You're right, Corey. Of course, you are. I just feel so . . . weird." Her gaze flickered self-consciously up. "More alone . . . if that makes any sense."

"What you need is a social life, love. I've told you that before." The air was rent with expectancy as Corey paused.

Whether Amber had hoped for just this line of conversation when she had rushed to Corey's place, she wasn't sure. It did fit in with her own way of thinking, after last night. "You may be right," she acknowledged with a knowing shrug.

"Look, love, I've mentioned this one guy before. He's great. Why don't you let me fix you up with him?"

Open-minded now, Amber faced her friend with interest. "Tell me about him."

Corey needed no more encouragement. "He is a doctor, in his late thirties. Divorced. I've met him at several medical meetings. He's tall, dark, and very good-looking. Well-mannered, interesting, dignified."

The description fit perfectly that of the man whose allure she was trying to escape by seeing other men. The coincidence would be too great, yet the medical community was a close-knit one. Amber had to satisfy the gnawing in the back of her mind. "And his name?"

"Zachary Wilder."

Her laugh held the hint of hysterics in its high pitch. "I can't believe that!"

Corey's eyes rounded as she misinterpreted her friend's reaction. "That *is* his name—what's so unbelievable?"

95

"Oh, Corey, it's not his name that's so incredible; it's just that I already . . . know . . . Zachary."

When the redhead perked up this time, it was in surprise. "You *know* him?" Then, her eyes narrowed as quickly. "You *know* him—exactly what do you mean by—know?" Amber's blush didn't escape her friend's notice. "Come on, spill it. You're holding out on me, Amber . . ." Her singsong tone trailed off, awaiting a reply.

Briefly, Amber outlined the occasions on which she and Zachary had met and spent time with one another, deliberately downplaying the attraction she felt for him and totally omitting the culmination of their date the evening before.

"So you *were* holding out on me," the other chided, reading more into Amber's veiled gaze than she was ready to confront.

"No, Corey, there was really nothing to tell you," she fibbed lightly. "Our paths just seem to keep crossing."

Corey's brows knit in puzzlement. "He's quite a man. Aren't you pleased that you keep bumping into him? He'd be a terrific companion."

"A little . . . overpowering." It was an understatement, but Amber's only concession to honesty. "You must know someone else . . . a little . . . less intense?"

It was the redhead's turn to laugh. "And here I thought I'd have to twist your arm! Sure, love, I'll find you a proper date," she assured her warmly. "Hold Wednesday night open. This one guy I have in mind will be off duty then."

Trying her best to ignore the second thoughts that had already begun to spring up, Amber smiled. "Wednesday night, it is."

Wednesday night it was, and a disaster from the word "go." The fellow was a pediatric cardiologist, a resident whom Corey had met at the hospital. He was, by all objective standards, prime material for a fun evening—handsome, witty, filled with energy. They spent the eve-

96

ning at a disco club, where he danced both himself and Amber ragged, as though letting off the steam of his more disciplined career. Where he managed to get the energy, when they finally left the place at midnight, to turn his attentions toward her, she didn't know. But suddenly she was in the hands of a lecher, fighting fingers that roamed her body irreverently, dodging lips that plundered in like manner—and all in the cramped front seat of his sporty, if somewhat battered, Karmann Ghia.

"Hey, babe, come on, loosen up!" he had ordered thickly, driven to passion by a mix of alcohol and Amber's undeniable attractiveness. For her part, there was nothing but revulsion, which she proceeded to outline for him in no uncertain terms, when he persisted in forcing his unwanted advances on her. The evening had ended soon after, but only after a few hurtful morsels had been thrown back at her. Fortunately, her recent responses to Zachary Wilder convinced her that she was neither an "ice maiden" nor "frigid." In fact, throughout the ordeal, her mind reverted repeatedly to the pleasure she had so recently found in Zachary's arms—and these thoughts made the present situation that much more offensive.

When Corey apologized profusely the following morning, Amber was quick to assure her that she had had no way of knowing the lusty intentions of her friend—and that no permanent harm had been done. In Amber's mind, the experience had convinced her that she was not merely sex-starved, which she had begun to wonder at one point the weekend before. Yet the dilemma remained of how to cope with her chemical reaction to Zachary. For the second time in a few short days, she dialed the phone again in search of an antidote.

"David," she began, having finally succeeded in locating her parents' friend at his home that evening, "you suggested, when we had dinner, that you had this client . . ." Awkwardly, she let her words trail off. It had been easier with Corey, who had actually broached the subject

97

herself. Unaccustomed to requests of this sort, Amber stumbled unsurely. "I—think I'd like—to go out—to have some fun . . ."

Mercifully, David Brigham followed her stammered words. Delighted, he jumped to her assistance. "You want that date I promised you! Good girl! This fellow is perfect for you." Then, hit by a brainstorm, he continued. "As a matter of fact, I'm having a group of people to the house on Saturday night. A very informal type of thing. Why don't you come? I'll introduce you to him there—assuming he's free."

Bidden by the same doubts she'd felt at Corey's, Amber pushed for more information. There was something terribly fateful about her previous encounters with one particular doctor, as though the two of them were destined to be thrown together. Hadn't her very decision to date other men been, in part, in response to this frightening sense of inevitability?

"What's his name, David?"

"Uh-uh," the voice on the line reproached her, "you'll just have to come and see. If he can't make it on Saturday, I'll give you a call. On second thought," he caught himself, "you come anyway! There will be any number of other interesting people for you to meet."

"I don't know, David—" she began in protest, one small part of her rebelling against the dubious wisdom of the entire plan.

"Well, I do, Amber. Trust me. This is the smartest thing you could be doing! Now, you just get yourself over here, looking as beautiful as you always do, and leave the rest to me. All right?"

The internal protest continued, but she heard her voice echo his "all right." As she hung up the phone, she wondered whether she was only asking for more trouble. At least, she reasoned, this time there would be the safety of a larger group of friendly people, with David to chaperone. And coming in her own car, there would be no repeat of the debacle of the evening before.

Friday morning brought the awareness, much as she fought its recognition, that she had heard nothing yet from Zachary. He had gone to Atlanta on Monday, with no word left as to the day of his anticipated return. Perhaps it was his absence which had given her the courage to go out on Wednesday night, though why she felt guilty about that, she didn't know. Arriving in her cubby of an office, laden with material on which she had worked at home, the thought crossed her mind to check with his office as to the date of his expected return. She had the perfect excuse, in the interview she'd had with him; it would be simple to tell his secretary that there were several points she had wanted to review before the final typing. In the end, pride kept her hand from the phone. If Zachary returned and wanted to see her, he could just contact her himself.

The last thing she expected was for it to happen that very morning. Head bent low over her work, she had momentarily blocked out all activity in the outer offices. The deep voice startled her from her concentration, demolishing it instantly.

"How are you, Amber?"

With a jerk, she straightened to find herself face-to-face with him. "Zachary!" she exclaimed, willing herself to keep calm and cool, "I didn't know you were back."

"I arrived early this morning and came directly to the hospital," he explained, his eyes deep blue and glittering. "Things have piled up during my absence. This is the first break I've had."

Throughout the week, Amber had steeled herself toward seeing him again, ever mindful of her vow that things had to be toned down between them. Now, however, the sight of him stirred an excitement in her that threatened to drive all thought of restraint from mind. Determinedly, she fought it.

"How—how did the trip go?" she asked, finding clear

99

thought suddenly more difficult, particularly when he propped himself on the edge of her desk. If he was at all tired from his trip and the hectic morning he must have had, there were no such signs on his ruggedly handsome face. He wore his customary hospital garb of a white jacket, parted now by the hand that thrust into the side pocket of his dark slacks, drawn snugly across the banded sinews of his thigh. The bronze sheen of his skin, the male set of his mouth, the patrician lines of his cheekbones and his nose, and the sensual depth of his eyes—all thrilled her as though for the first time. That those last, his eyes, remained locked into hers and made no move to skim her with anything akin to sexuality, relaxed her, bolstering her own attempt at evenness.

"It was productive. My lecture was received well. Hopefully, we may have won some supporters for the cause."

"The International Center?" It was easier to maintain her composure when the discussion dealt with the hospital.

"Ummm. There were representatives from medical centers all over the country. I've sometimes worried that more of our support came from foreigners, when we need every last bit of the American following too."

The apparent success of his trip brought a genuine smile to her lips. "That's great! Is there anything I can add to this brochure?"

The darkness of his head tilted to allow him sight of the papers on her desk. When he leaned forward, her pulse speeded. "Not yet," he murmured softly. "But"—he raised his eyes to hers by way of her lips—"you could join me for lunch."

Reason commanded that she refuse his invitation. "I don't know, Zachary. I've got so much to do in the next hour before I leave for the day." The argument sounded weak, even to her—as though she were merely angling for further encouragement.

100

The sonorous timbre of his response indulged her. "Come on, Amber. You could use a break, too. You'll just stay a few minutes later." Humor lurked in his gaze, challenging her to maintain that there was other business that afternoon which could not be put off.

Reason was quickly cast aside, as she was all too prone to do in his presence. "You seem to have all the answers," she murmured softly, flashing a shy smile in his direction. Leaning over to retrieve her pocketbook, she rose and followed him out of the office.

Lunch in the hospital cafeteria was at once the most pleasant and most agonizing experience she had had. Zachary sat beside her at a small table, leaning intimately close to her ear to talk and be heard over the steady drone of conversation surrounding him. If his words were impersonal, the presence of his long, lean body beside her was not. Reduced to a mass of raw nerve endings, she could only pick at her tuna salad, acutely aware of the strength of the thigh that rested against hers, flexing periodically beneath the table. When she raised her eyes in warning, his own told her that he knew exactly what he was doing and its profound effect on her, yet he somehow managed to keep the flow of conversation on that same innocent tone he had maintained in her office. It was only as they stood to leave, and his hand closed about the slimness of her upper arm, that she sensed his behavior had backfired.

Out of desperation, she began to pull away when they reached the long white corridor. "I'll find my way back to the office. Thank you for lunch." But the hand on her arm tightened and he kept apace with her. His motive in studying the doors on either side, as they passed, eluded her. She was taken totally off guard when he reached for one and drew her with lightning speed into a small utility closet.

"What—" The rest of her words were absorbed by his mouth, which clamped over hers forcefully, as the door closed to leave them in darkness. Instinctively, she protested, squirming from his grasp, only to find herself captured and held against the wall by the firmness of his body.

"Hold still," he ordered, his voice low and husky. "I've wanted to do this since I laid eyes on you this morning. It's been a very long week."

His words held the ring of truth, for both of them. Amber had spent the majority of the week trying to push thoughts of him from mind—with little success. The memory of the fervor of his lips on hers, playing havoc with her senses, had haunted her, only to return now in vivid rebirth. But what of her vows, of her determination to avoid a repeat of their heady encounter? The nearness of him, the intimacy of his body against hers, the scent of clean maleness that tantalized her—all dulled her reserve.

When his lips descended to repossess her mouth, she struggled with the last remnants of sanity, holding her lips together tightly, stiffening her body against his onslaught. But it was useless. The initial force of his kiss gentled to a warm persuasiveness which overpowered her, sending shudders of delight racing along her spine. When his arms slid behind her back to draw her against him, she gave up the fight, yielding to the temptation of the pleasure of his masculinity.

Waves of sensation coursed through her veins, sending her arms creeping up, over his shoulders and into the thickness of the dark hair at the nape of his neck. With a sigh of ecstasy, she allowed him to part her lips and deepen the kiss. His tongue darted into the recesses of her mouth, thrilling her with each thrust. Slowly she responded, helpless in his arms. When his body crushed hers more tightly, she realized that it was the pressure of her own arms that encouraged the movement. The equilibrium she had tried so hard to maintain was a far memory, holding no place in the emotional quake that rocked her.

"Ah," he groaned against the corner of her mouth, "that's better." His hands shimmied down to the small of her back, arching her against his manly lines until she caught her breath at his arousal.

"It won't be, in a minute," she warned laughingly, her breath coming in strangely hoarse gasps. "I've got to be getting back to work . . ."

To her instant regret, his arms slackened their hold, easing her back against the wall as his hands straddled it, his forehead resting against hers, his breathing unsteady. "You're right, little lady. A good coach. Very effective."

When he made no move to leave the closet, she chided him softly. "What if someone walks in here, Zachary. Your reputation . . ."

". . . is that of the lady killer. It would only confirm what most of the nurses whisper on their coffee breaks, anyway."

"Is that so?" The darkness hid her arched brow, though not the pointed teasing of her question.

His breath fanned the escaped strands of hair by her temple. "Jealous?"

"Who, me?" she retorted, too quickly. She was to wonder about that later, but, for now, there was only the problem of returning to a more sober state.

His subsequent gruffness puzzled her. "Forget I asked that. Listen, how about going out with me tomorrow night? We could go somewhere nice for dinner—"

"I can't, Zachary. I already have plans." Though she knew it was for the best, she was momentarily sorry she had agreed to meet David Brigham's mysterious client.

Even in the darkness, his frown chilled her, accompanied by the imperceptible tensing of his limbs as he straightened. "I thought you didn't 'date'?" The accusation was made in a voice suddenly cooled.

"I don't," she hastened back, "not frequently anyway." She was puzzled by his tension, simultaneously pleased and disturbed by the possessive quality of his manner. "It's j—just a party—"

"With many an eligible man around."

"Perhaps." She had been independent for too long to idly submit to his implication.

Tautly stretched lips mocked her word "perhaps." But the leering note in his tone carried an emotion she could not fathom. Within moments, she was escorted back into the hall and toward her office, the return walk accomplished in an awkward silence. His only parting words were an indifferent "have fun," then he disappeared from the door and back the way he had come, his face drawn into a mask of studied calm.

The next day, Saturday, dragged on with agonizing slowness. Maddeningly, Amber's thoughts retraced the events of the Saturday before, which had been filled with fun and pleasure. Zachary had been every bit the warm and stimulating companion, easygoing and understanding. The chill with which he had left her yesterday was out of character with the man she thought she knew. The memory of his indifference continued to baffle her. Was he angry? Unsure? Jealous? What was his great objection to the idea that she might see other men? After all, their own dating relationship had been barely established. Was his pride hurt? He had seemed so much more confident and strong; to lower himself to that kind of male arrogance did not befit the image she had built in her mind of him. Had she been wrong? Had she misjudged his true character?

Interspersed with these questions was the one filled with self-reproach. After those days of warning herself to resist his physical charms, she had capitulated fully and willingly. Why? What was it about the man, this one particular man, that devastated her? What was the nature of the power he held over her the instant he stepped close? For, she realized, she not only had him to fear, but herself. She could be her own worst enemy, quivering mindlessly in the embrace of this enigmatic man. How could she deal with him?

Distasteful as she found the thought of attending this

party at David's, she saw it as a necessity. Circulation was the word; if she wanted to meet other men, she had to make herself available. And, yes, if this one client whom David had in mind for her was not to her liking, there would certainly be others at the party. If worst came to worst, she could contrive return invitations from those potential beaux whom she had refused in the past. Some of them weren't all *that* bad, she tried to convince herself, with negligible success.

For the party, she chose a lavender wrap dress of a soft crepe material. The waist, sashed and slim, gave way to a pleated fullness that mirrored the puff sleeves which gathered just above the elbow. The open vee neck slashed to a respectable depth, showing off the beige skin of her throat and the coral necklace she wore to perfection. Determined to project an air of maturity and sophistication, she wound the long silken strands of her blond tresses in a chic coil at the back of her head, fastening tiny coral studs on her earlobes and a thin coral bracelet about her wrist. Her makeup was applied with care, again to create the understated image of allure. With a last dab of perfume behind her ears, on her wrists, and in the provocative hollow between her breasts, she was off.

David Brigham was the consummate host, greeting her warmly at the door of his large Tudor home in affluent Chestnut Hill, leading her from guest to guest in proper introductory fashion, finally leaving her with several other singles to attend to a newer arrival. "Your fellow isn't here yet," he murmured softly in her ear before he left. "He said he'd be slightly delayed, but that he would be here." With a pat to her elbow and a smile of encouragement, he moved on.

To her surprise, Amber found herself relaxed and interested in the conversation of the group. One of the men, a stockbroker in his midthirties, was particularly charming, deliberately drawing her into the discussion with the two others, a pair of academicians, man and woman, who seemed to be attached to each other in some way, though Amber could not quite figure out how. Nonetheless, they were pleasant company, complementing the polished words of the stockbroker with their own ivory-tower ideology. As the minutes passed, Amber nearly forgot that there was one guest, yet to arrive, for whom she was intended. Her enjoyment of the nascent evening was etched in the gentleness of the smile on her face, when David touched her elbow lightly, to attract her attention and finally introduce her to his late-arriving client. Turning, her gaze riveted instantly to one that she knew all too well.

"Zachary!" she whispered, cursing herself for not having insisted that David identify him on the phone. It was one coincidence too many. Embarrassment washed over her. Excitement surged through her. Annoyance blunted her nerve endings. Astonishment rendered further speech impossible. In short, a gaping abyss of emotional confusion threatened to swallow her up—until she was saved by the calm and courteous greeting of the tall man before her.

"You look beautiful, Amber. It's good to see you again."

CHAPTER SIX

"Do you two know each other?" David's question and his obvious surprise broke through Amber's daze, abruptly reminding her of her host's presence which she had momentarily forgotten. Her eyes flew to his in confusion; again, she was rescued by the handsome doctor.

"We have had an opportunity to work together recently at the hospital," the deep voice explained with ultimate composure, so opposite to Amber's own tongue-tied state. A gracious smile curved his lips, yet failed to reach his eyes. "I'm pleased to have the chance to see her again." His gaze, which had grown more piercing by the minute, finally shifted toward their host. "How did you happen to come across such a lovely woman, David?"

Even as Amber silently thanked Zachary for these precious moments he allowed her to regain her poise, she sensed an undercurrent of sarcasm in his words. Defensively, she lowered her head, studying the crisscross of her sandal straps as she awaited David's response.

"I represent Amber, much as I do you, Zach. Actually, we've known each other for years." He looked quickly at Amber, puzzled by her discomfiture. Pure fondness for her brought forth his follow-up. "Her parents are good friends of mine. I can remember when she was so high," he sliced his hand at waist height, "and managed to wrap me around her baby finger." The laughter just below the surface of his words brought Amber's blond head up, her cheeks flaming brightly.

"David . . ." she warned gently, finding her voice enough to plead subtly that he discontinue that particular line of conversation. But in this case, Zachary was all too eager to hear more, rather enjoying her embarrassment.

"Tell me more, friend," he coaxed the attorney through his broad smile. "Was she a spitfire then too?"

To Amber's consternation, her old friend seemed as willing to join in the game. "Spitfire, tomboy, mischiefmaker . . . but ever the tease." Offered so innocently, his words were agony to her.

"David," she burst out softly, trying to feign the indignance which indeed she felt, "you're giving away all my secrets. That was a long time ago." Total anger at her friend would not come; his warmly indulgent expression precluded it. But he had no way of knowing how disturbing this talk was to her—in front of Zachary Wilder.

It was the rich baritone that suddenly was all too close to her ear. "So she's finally found her tongue again. Perhaps a little goading here and there is all it takes," he teased, exchanging a wicked grin with his male accomplice.

Amber envisioned the game, now, with the two men throwing a ball back and forth, delighted at her inability to catch it. Competitive by nature, however, she recognized when she was outmatched. Drawing the corners of her lips down in disgust, she propped her slender fingers on her hips and adopted that very role of the spitfire. "All right, you two. If all you care to do is to tease me, I can find more interesting companionship elsewhere." Then, pasting a most polite expression on her still-flushed face, she said, "If you'll excuse me . . ." With an equally polite nod of her head, she turned and gracefully moved to the opposite side of the room, willing her legs to carry her steadily, despite their infuriating shakiness.

Finding herself at the bar, she quickly ordered a gin and tonic, inhaling deeply to calm herself as the bartender mixed her drink. Cool glass in hand, she headed for the nearest group of people, none of whom she had yet met, and, with a forwardness inspired by sheer desperation, she boldly introduced herself and joined the conversation. Outwardly, it was more easily accomplished than she had expected, for the talk of the group—which included several lawyers and their wives, or dates, or acquaintances of that same evening, she wasn't sure which—was of the economy, particularly the state of the tax situation in Massachusetts, which involved her directly as well. Inwardly, it was another matter. For her thoughts lingered at that other side of the room, where she had left David and Zachary, wondering what they had said to one another when she had left, wondering why Zachary hadn't followed her, wondering why he had let her go in the first place. Then, she caught herself up short, appalled by the train of her thoughts.

She had come here to meet new people, to "cure" herself of Zachary Wilder, just as she had tried to do on that abominable date with the wild-handed cardiologist not so long ago. And, to think, that the very man David had had in mind for her was Zachary—the thread of coincidence threatened to strangle her. All roads seemed to lead back to him. Was it fate? Conspiracy? Destiny? Even as she made pretense of interest in the discussion at hand, her eye darted surreptitiously, and with as much nonchalance as possible, around the room in search of the tall dark doctor. When his handsome head came into view, it was bent in discussion with a beautiful woman, a tall and slender black-haired vision. There was no denying, this time, that the knot in her stomach was formed by jealousy. Angered, she threw herself even more actively into her present company, trying desperately to immerse herself into their conversation, succeeding dismally, and hating herself for it. When the stockbroker, with whom she had been speaking earlier, appeared at her elbow, she welcomed the change.

His suggestion that they walk out onto the terrace seemed a wise one, removing her as it would from the confines of this room where Zachary's presence haunted her. Bearing her eyes straight ahead, tossing an occasional smile to her escort as they made their way around various clusters of people toward the sliding glass doors, now open, she saw no sign of that dark head. Yet, as soon as she relaxed into a cushioned patio chair, with the stockbroker right beside her, she knew why. There, not fifteen feet from where they sat, was Zachary, charming a couple, man and woman, with some story. At least, she breathed a sigh of relief, the couple were together—that was more palatable. But as she turned to face her own companion, the same gorgeous raven-haired beauty smoothly glided over the flagstone to take her place at Zachary's side—and Amber's composure was threatened anew. All too often she had wondered about conspiracy; now she did again. Why, or what, was it that persisted in dangling this magnificent man before her? And why, oh why, did he disturb her so? After all, it was *she* who had refused his offer of a date for this evening. She could have been out with him, alone—her heart lurched at the thought. No, she reasoned feebly, this was the much safer way. Determinedly, she focused her attention on the stockbroker, who, by comparison, suddenly threatened to bore her to tears.

By midevening, when a light buffet was served in David's spacious dining room, Amber had had enough of the entire party. Yet, courtesy and pride kept her smiling and pretending fascination with the various other people whom David graciously presented to her. That her host made no quiet mention of her reaction to Zachary puzzled her, though this, she knew, was neither the time nor the place for such reckoning. Zachary did not approach her, and was kept busy himself with a never-ending stream of company. She could not keep her eyes from periodically seeking him out, yet not once did she find his eyes on her. Hurt, confused, and disappointed, particularly in light of the intimacy they had shared, she struggled to steel herself. It was her specialty, wasn't it? she asked herself.

"Ah, Amber, there you are." It was David, approaching from behind, who drew her attention to a young man, blond-haired and tanned, dressed more casually than the others in a lightweight blazer, plaid shirt, and jeans, and very good-looking. "This is Andrew Pasco. He is a photographer, free-lance. You two should have a lot in common."

In the instant, Amber was inspired. So there *was* a way to get into the game after all! A photographer, young, rakishly handsome, and just the one to take her mind from that more mature dark figure! "I'm very pleased to meet you, Andrew." She smiled warmly, extending her hand to be grasped by his firm one.

"The pleasure's mine, Amber." The gray of his eyes echoed the greeting, encouraging her in her scheme. "You have very good taste in women, David." He turned back to their host for a minute, before the latter excused himself and moved on, leaving Amber to her wiles, which she proceeded to exercise with daring skill. She conversed animatedly with the young man as they both munched on the gastronomical offerings, then moved back to a corner of the living room to continue talking. He was both friendly and interesting, possessing a spontaneity which had been tethered in many of the others she had met that evening. For a few minutes, she actually did manage to push thoughts of Zachary from mind, being caught up happily in her own game. Andrew was a delightful conversationalist, and they did, indeed, have much in common, discussing both photography and journalism for the better part of the next hour. If she had come to the party to meet people—and potential dating material—her purpose was accomplished in Andrew. Yet, when it appeared that he would ask her out, she hesitated instinctively—but only for a moment, for the sight, out of the corner of her eye, of Zachary staring at her over the head of his lovely companion, reminded her of her intent. When Andrew proposed an evening of theater at the Loeb, she promptly

111

accepted, mentally chalking off that next Saturday night more as necessity than desire.

"Can I give you a lift home?" the blond-haired photographer asked softly, invitingly, when the guests began to take their leave.

Fortunately, Amber had a ready excuse. "Oh, I've got my own car here, Andrew. But thank you. And I will see you next Saturday?"

"You bet, pretty lady," he confirmed the date with a wink, walking with her to find and thank David for his hospitality, then seeing her safely to her car. It was, all in all, a pleasant ending to an evening that could have been totally disastrous. Yet, once alone and covering the roads back toward Dover, the torment of rationalization swallowed her up.

You've done the right thing, she told herself over and over and over again, fighting to overcome the uneasy feeling that raged as the reality of the situation became clear. But was it right—to use this very nice fellow for her own purposes? For she *was* using him, to dull the impact of Zachary Wilder on her senses. Yes, Andrew was charming and their date would, no doubt, be enjoyable, yet she felt none of the instant attraction for him that Zachary inspired. With relief, she acknowledged that her reference was not solely toward the world of passion the dark doctor had awakened. Andrew Pasco was as good-looking, in his way, yet his grasp of her hand as he led her from room to room, his touch on her back as he opened her car door for her, unleashed none of the fire that the other man had. There was, indeed, though, more to the comparison than mere physical desire. Andrew, interesting as was his career, lacked the maturity, the stability, the overall sense of commitment that Zachary mastered.

Stability? Commitment? Working double-time, Amber's mind flew one step further and she gasped aloud, swerving to avoid a fallen branch in the road which her preoccupation had prevented her from seeing earlier.

112

What did she want with stability, with commitment? Exactly what was it she sought? Chagrined, she realized that her comparisons of Zachary with other men had evolved to the point of thought of a husband. *A husband? Marriage?* Hadn't she been down that road before? Yet, much as she fought the idea, Zachary embodied all of those things that she might have considered ideal in a husband, a life-mate, a lover.

As she turned into the drive and parked her car in front of the garage, the maelstrom of emotion which this man had the knack of creating in her grew to torment her once more. Angrily, she bounded from the car, slammed its door with a loud bang, and stormed into the house, dropping her things in heaps on the sofa, dashing upstairs to throw herself under a cold shower in hopes of regaining some of the good sense on which she had prided herself for the past four years. The attempt was futile; the harsh pelting of the water did nothing to harden her to the emotions she felt, nor did the warmer stream she next resorted to help to ease her tension. It seemed that only one man was capable of doing that, and he had spent the evening entranced by a very attentive woman.

Just barely toweling her body and her dripping hair, she threw on her short terry robe and headed aimlessly back downstairs, knowing that, despite the lateness of the hour, sleep would be elusive. A thunderous banging on the front door startled her before she had even reached the bottom step. The sound of the doorknob rattling back and forth terrified her. Who could be here at this hour and with such obvious impatience? Torn between running to phone the police and peering through the front window to see who the intruder might be, the decision was rendered unnecessary.

"Amber! Open up the damn door!"

His voice was instantly recognizable, even with its unfamiliar anger. Her bare foot hesitated on the bottom step for just a moment as she took a deep breath, then slowly padded to the door.

"Where in the devil were you? I've been banging on this door for the past ten minutes!" He seemed a giant, towering furiously over her, his blue eyes dark and accusing. Yet, as she stepped back to allow his entrance, she was neither frightened nor indignant. She had wanted, all evening, to be with him; that she knew, without a doubt.

"I was in the shower." Her voice was a soft whisper, apologetic in a strange and unnecessary way.

The door slammed behind him. "So I can see!" he bellowed, taking in her damp appearance with one sweeping, knowing, provocative glance. While she knew she should be angry at his presumption that she answer the door at his first knock, there was nothing but a strong sense of satisfaction that surged through her body, the familiar yearnings for this man tingling into life at his very survey of her. Having no retort for him, she merely stood back and watched him stalk into the room, his eye settling on her haphazard pile of clothing before returning to her.

"Are you alone?"

His harsh words stilled those growing flames instantly. Shocked at his insinuation and deeply hurt, she stared at him, her eyes flickering their green shards in rounded pools. Her expression was answer to his question; determinedly, she held her tongue, then thought twice about doing so. Impulsively, she threw back her own barb.

"I'm surprised *you* are! You seemed to have quite an attentive and willing companion at the party."

For the first time since he'd entered, a light of humor entered his eye, but only briefly, before it was replaced by the same fierceness that seemed now to possess him in entirety. "I don't know how you ever managed to notice, occupied as *you* were with that young . . . lad."

"He happened to have been very interesting," she said in defense of her new friend, "and since there was no one else as fascinating to talk with . . ."

114

"Thank you for the compliment. I'll remember it." His glare left no doubt as to his interpretation of her words, yet her own resentment of his avoidance of her prevented her from enlightening him.

"You do that, next time you see your dark-haired friend! And what, might I ask, are you doing here now? Making sure that I have my door locked?" Her reference to his earlier instructions was not lost on him.

"You damned well better leave your door locked, Amber. If you've suddenly decided to date men, be prepared for what they want from you. You're far too alluring for the average man to resist for very long."

"But you're not the average man, are you?" she screamed back, driven by her own burgeoning frustration. "You can resist me any time you want. I can feel perfectly safe with you, can't I?" Immediately, she regretted her words, for he took several strides toward her, the gleam in his eye no longer from anger, but rather born of a more primal intent. What drove her on, she would never know. "I just don't understand you, Zachary. You ignore me all evening and then barge in here, incensed at something which totally escapes me."

He stood mere inches from her now, though he made no move to touch her. "Escapes you? You have no idea why I'm angry? I asked you out for tonight, to be with me and me alone, not to spend the evening with thirty other predominantly boring people." Hadn't the same thoughts gone through her own head more than once that evening? Yet, it did not excuse his anger. Had he approached her once, only once, that night and suggested they take off together somewhere, she would have gone willingly. But he hadn't. So what did he want now? The light in his eye told her, though she wanted, needed to hear him say it.

Suddenly, his nearness began to affect her deeply. The way his hair fell, so darkly, across his forehead, the way his tie had been loosened and his top buttons undone to reveal those tantalizing dark tufts of hair on his chest, the very male scent of him which eroded her resentment—stumbling from him, she tried to escape to the far side of the room. But a firm hand snaked out and caught at her damp hair, hauling her back to him, bringing memories of that first day she had met him.

Wincing with pain, her hand shot up to her scalp. "What do you want from me, Zachary?"

He didn't hesitate. "I don't want you to flaunt your charms to every man available—and in my presence particularly."

"I don't belong to you and you have no reason to be jealous . . ." Both statements were true, yet one conflicted with the other in ways that were obvious to them both. The savage grimace which contorted his handsome features did frighten her for an instant, as his hands settled on her shoulders with brute strength.

"I am jealous, damn it! I don't want to have to stand across a room and look at you all night without doing this—" His words died against her lips when his head swooped low. Resisting his anger, she held her lips taut, pushing against the wall of his chest with the palms of her hands. This was a Zachary Wilder she did not know—this forceful hulk of a man. Yet, even as it bewildered her, there was an inexplicable excitement, both in his force and his possessiveness. His mouth covered hers, plundering the rigid set of her own, forcing an entry that she was determined to resist despite the flicker of flames within her. His hands dug into her shoulders, biting through the terry fabric, then suddenly they slackened and he drew his head up to look at her. Could he see the well of emotion in her eyes, a force her lips had denied?

Slowly and now gently, his large hands raised to frame her face, his thumbs caressing the moist outline of her lips. This was the lure she could not resist; perhaps he knew that. This tenderness, this understanding, this gentle persuasion was her undoing. With a low moan, a culmination of the evening's frustration, she parted her lips against his thumbs, kissing them lightly and instinctively. This was what she craved, she cried silently, as her fingers glided up the length of his shirt-sleeve to his shoulders. When he lowered his head a second time, she held nothing back, robbed of all resistance by the intoxication of his manliness. Her mouth opened into his, tasting his tongue and tracing his teeth with her own. The sparks of passion ignited further when his hands dropped to touch her, exploring the curves of her body through her robe, lingering at every hill and hollow. A gasp quivered from the back of his throat when he realized that she wore nothing beneath the robe. Fiercely, he hugged her to him, as though trying to absorb her body into his despite all barriers.

Amber felt an erotic heat pour through her, frustrated as he was by those very barriers. The soft words of love at her ear were intermingled with nips and tugs of his teeth on her lobe, driving her further to distraction. She needed more, and she sought it. The urge to touch him was too intense to deny. When she levered herself back to touch his neck, to let the manly hair on his chest curl beneath her fingers, he had the outlet he needed. His hand released the belt of her robe, his fingers slid beneath its lapels.

For a breathless minute, she froze. Her hands clutched the fabric protectively about her, as her rounded eyes caught his. "Zach . . . I . . . I don't know . . ."

The silence was more potent than any words he might have spoken. He held her gaze, hypnotizing her with the force of his all-encompassing virility. Slowly, slowly, sanity receded, and her hands drifted away. The white terry fabric slid down her body to lie in a half-circle at her feet.

Naked now before him, she caught her breath and would have reflexively tried to cover herself had not his hands held her arms from her sides. But embarrassment faded to pleasure, then pride, as his eyes roamed her feminine form, caressing her breasts, her flat belly, then lower,

117

feasting on the sight of her, from head to toe for the first, divine time.

He said nothing, yet her knees trembled at his visual seduction. Slowly, he let his hands wander, savoring the softness of her skin, then curving behind her back and beneath her bottom to lift her off her feet and cross the few feet to the sofa, where he lay her down then sat beside her. "You're very beautiful and warm, my Amber," he murmured thickly, his fingers foraying into every secret spot until she writhed with pleasure and desire.

The throbbing within her grew by the minute, as her blood ran a passionate race through her veins. She was a pagan goddess being worshipped by her god, himself a magnificent creature to behold. All reason vanished. The only thought was that she wanted to feel him, too, to adore him, to know his hard man's body against hers. Trembling hands released the buttons of his shirt, tugged at his loosened tie, then stilled as he finished the job himself, discarding the clothing carelessly on the floor. His chest was warm and sinewed, broad, but lean and strong. Flames soared within her when he stretched out beside her on the sofa, touching her, teasing her, tormenting her to forgetfulness. Her own hands searched further, discovering newer spots to relish, finally creeping lower to move up and down his muscled thigh, timidly at first, but with the dire need to touch him. He was bold and full and strong, moaning as she caressed him, muttering a soft oath, at last, before hastily reaching for the buckle of his belt.

As she watched him lower the zipper of his pants, Amber knew that she wanted Zachary more than she'd ever wanted any other man. She wanted him to make love to her, to possess her completely. More than that, she wanted to say the words that surged from within, the words that she never thought she'd ever say again to a man. As she lay, naked before him, waiting for his own nakedness to bring her his personal ecstasy, she knew that

118

she wanted to hear those same words from him. But it was not to be.

A shrill buzzer sounded from the direction of the chair on which he had tossed his jacket when he'd first entered. All action stopped, though his eyes did not leave the loveliness of her body as he let reality intrude, slowly but repeatedly, on their lovemaking.

"Damn it!" he swore beneath his breath, rezipping his pants and going to retrieve the buzzer. "It's the hospital. They'd only buzz me if it was an emergency. I'll have to call in." His voice was hoarse, his arousal as painfully obvious as Amber's own. The hand that crossed his dampened forehead was impatient, as were the steps which took him out to the kitchen to use the phone.

Alone, Amber's trembling increased, fed by shock, desire, and, worse, shame. Yes, she wanted to say those words, but did she dare? Did she love Zachary? Driven by desire, she would have willingly given herself to him, had not he once more—albeit spurred by outside forces—called a halt to it. Shakily, she retrieved her robe and drew it around her, tying the belt with fierce finality. Then, sinking down once more upon the sofa, she hung her head and, to her chagrin, buried her face in her hands and began to cry. Confusion overwhelmed her; she had been senseless once more in Zachary's arms. What was she to do?

"There's an emergen—Amber?" She hadn't heard him return, so immersed was she in her own emotional upheaval. "What is it, honey?" he asked, coming down to a squat before her, his hands on her knees. "Don't cry, please, Amber." But sobs continued to rack her body until he took her in his arms and held her tightly. "What is it? Please tell me? I'd have been back—"

"I—I'm so ashamed," she croaked between sobs. "I never should have done that . . ."

"Shhh," he crooned softly, holding her, hugging her, burying her wet face against the textured chest that moments before she had caressed with abandon. "You have nothing to be ashamed of, honey. Please believe that. You're a woman with a woman's body and a great deal of passion to give. You can't imagine how much I want you." But that wasn't what Amber wanted to hear. When he held her back a moment later, she felt a stabbing pain sear through her. "There's been a bad accident. The emergency room is loaded with victims—a bus ran off the Expressway and fell twenty feet. They need every doctor they can get their hands on. I'll have to go." His eyes held hers with lingering passion mixed with regret, but her own pain raged on. "I'll probably be there for the night. Can I see you tomorrow?"

"No, Zachary." She heard the voice of reason which had been driven to oblivion by his masterful persuasion earlier. "I need time . . . to think . . ."

For long moments, he searched her face for a sign of her thoughts. Then, with a ragged sigh and a hand combed roughly through his hair, he stood. "I'm having a meeting at my house on Tuesday night of a group of local doctors regarding the International Center. Why don't you come?" The blue of his eyes had a pleading note that the evenness of his voice disguised. "I could use a hostess."

Perhaps you could use a wife, a small voice inside her cried, then stifled itself reproachfully. The issue was a sore one for her. Having been such a dismal failure of a wife for one man in one respect, who was she to suggest anything to another, let alone to herself? "I don't know," she finally murmured, her words mirroring the far larger dilemma which, at the moment, precluded any rational decision. Her eye followed his deft movement as Zachary bent to retrieve his shirt, then put it on, the ripple of arm and chest muscles mesmerizing her anew. The low sound of his voice startled her back to the present.

"You'd find it interesting, and you might be able to pick up a few points for your brochures and the larger report the department is doing." His deep blue eyes studied her as he awaited a response, his jaw tensed and unusually angular, his hands independently buttoning his shirt and stuffing its tails into his pants. Beneath the closeness of his gaze, Amber felt herself a sad sight, hair snarled still from her shower, eyes now tear-ravaged, face devoid of color or makeup. Averting her eyes, she struggled to gain control over her emotions and the situation, resorting to the crisp wit which had worked for her in the past.

"Do I get time-and-a-half for overtime?"

Her attempt at humor fell flat. Burdened both by his own frustration and anticipation of the night ahead, Zachary was in no mood for her witticism. His face was inscrutable as he grabbed his tie and jacket and headed for the door. "The meeting is set for eight. Try to make it." No further word was spoken, either of demand or encouragement. Amber's fine-tuned ear heard the front door close firmly, the rapid charge of footsteps down the walk to the drive, the smooth purr of the BMW engine into life, then the fading hum of its departure. Strangely cold and empty, she headed for bed.

The night was dark, its barrenness intensifying her feelings of confusion and desolation as she lay in bed, unable to sleep. There were no light images on the walls or ceilings to soften the pictures her mind drew both of past and present. Of only one thing was she certain—that Zachary Wilder meant far more to her than she was ready to admit, much as she had wanted to earlier that evening. The extent of her abandonment, then, shocked her afresh. Indeed, with neither promise of love nor future, her traitorous body would have drawn his into it gladly. Now, with the cooling of the ardor that had engulfed her, she was horrified at what she might have done. She had only given herself to one man before, and he had been her husband. Zachary was not her husband, and could hardly be in love with her, having been burned once at the altar. That he wanted her physically was clear. Now, he wanted her to "hostess" a meeting with him. Exactly what did that mean in terms of their relationship?

Her wandering mind conjured images of the tanned chest on which she had lain her head, the firm shoulder muscles over which her fingertips had played, the proof of manhood which her hand had discovered at every swell and plane of his body. The familiar trembling began once more, an echo of the stirring in her loins that spoke as much of her own needs as his that had been more visible. In the instant, Amber knew it was inevitable; one day they *would* make love, as Zachary had promised that last Saturday night. For her, she knew, it would be a magnificent happening. But for him? *Would* she be able to satisfy him, as she had evidently been unable to do for Ron? It was a nagging insecurity that her ex-husband had bequeathed her, yet, in Zachary's arms, she forgot it totally. He had the power to make her believe in herself and in him. Did she love him? Did she love him? Did she love him?

As many times as the question was asked, its answer remained elusive. In the end, Amber abandoned it, concentrating on the more urgent issue of whether or not to attend his meeting on Tuesday night. He was right—it would be a good thing to sit in on, considering the line of her own work. But what would it lead to? Whereas when she had first met him, Zachary had seemed so smooth and even-tempered, in their last few encounters he had shown a proclivity toward temper that had startled her. Deep within her was a desire to please him, a need to please him, a kind of giving of her own. Did her presence counteract that desire? Would she be better to avoid him completely?

A bittersweet laugh filtered from her throat into the still of the night, a harsh sound in contrast to the soft drops of rain that had begun a slow-tempo dance on the roof above her head. To avoid Zachary Wilder would be next to impossible. All fates seemed to throw them together, regardless of their own wishes. And as for her wish? Her heart could not possibly avoid him, as long as he was present and caring and so much in command of the feminine instinct which craved fulfillment.

* * *

That feminine instinct was not to find fulfillment at the home of Zachary Wilder on Tuesday night. As one part of her had known from the moment he had mentioned the meeting, she *did* attend it. The house was a ten-minute drive from her own, in an even more rural area of Dover, deeply forested, with large fields interspersed occasionally from one private drive to another. The sun had begun to lower for the night, spilling its orange glow through the verdant growth, across the roads, and, finally, over the front of his home, as it burst into view at the end of a long driveway. If her own was one of those nine out of ten old houses, his was not. Fully contemporary, from wood and glass front and sides to multiple skylights overhead, its concession to mankind was minimal, blending gracefully with the natural setting all about it, giving one the feeling, when within, of being, indeed, without.

Zachary was the perfect host, behaving toward her in as charming a manner as he was gracious to the others. Though he introduced her around at the start of the meeting, she received no further attention as one who was an outsider, so to speak. Her hand made note after note as the group of doctors talked. There were twelve of them, including two women whose status immediately put Amber in her place. Her eye fell on these two more often than on the others, with the exception of their leader. What did they think of him ... as a man, she wondered? What were his thoughts about their own not inconsiderable feminine traits? Both were attractive and well-spoken, intelligent, and seemingly respected by the others in the group. Was there a special glow in Zachary's eye when either of them spoke? Had he ever dated either one?

Such questions spilled one after the other through her brain as the meeting continued, then appeared to be winding up. Suddenly, she heard mention of her own name.

"Mrs. MacLaine"—*did he emphasize that Mrs. more so than necessary?* she wondered idly—"has been working on

123

our PR material. Perhaps you could give us a quick run-down on the progress to date, Amber." His blue eyes bore a challenge, as though he had been completely aware of her mental aberrations and found some enjoyment in jolting her from them.

Calling on every bit of her poise and composure, Amber rose to the occasion, both literally and figuratively. Determined, in the instant, to make the most of this opportunity both to push Zachary's cause and to impress him with her ability to do so, she stood and moved slowly—and with a show of confidence that went no further than that lovely surface—to where Zachary had been standing, to where he now sat in a large easy chair. Placing herself just to his right, close enough to identify with him yet far enough for propriety, she spoke, outlining concisely the overall plan of the fund-raising drive, describing the preliminary brochures that had already been sent to the printer, elaborating more fully on the major report on which the bulk of her efforts was centered at this point. She sought eye contact wherever possible, making her delivery crisp and effective. The several questions that came to her were handled with similar ease, justifying the long hours she had spent at home poring over every last bit of material she had regarding the project and the fund-raising drive.

"Very effective, coach." Zachary approached from behind while she stood talking with one of the other doctors moments later, when coffee and danish had been served in the large dining area at one end of the very open living room. "I'll have to call on your talents again at my meetings."

There was definite humor in his voice, though Amber's mind blotted it out. Excusing herself from the man with whom she had been speaking, she turned to face the tall and commanding host. "You certainly didn't need a hostess here, that's for sure. You make a very good cup of coffee." What she felt inside, she wasn't sure. There was warmth and sarcasm, jealousy and admiration, attraction

124

and resentment—a whole gamut of conflicts that his presence evoked. Yet, when he smiled, the even whiteness of his teeth so fresh and tempting to the tip of her tongue, she melted.

"I've had to learn to do many things myself. But I really did want you to come. Thank you." He paused, his eye reinforcing that sentiment with a beam that seared into her, wrapping itself around her heart, which beat suddenly faster. "Have you been able to get any information you can use?" His dark head cocked toward the notebook she still held under her arm.

"I think so. I'll have to read over my notes when I get home. There was a lot that was said—it will take some sorting out."

Zachary's nod preceded a silence that was anticipatory of something—then fell flat when one of the woman doctors approached. "Very interesting, Zach!" she congratulated him spiritedly, linking her elbow with his in an all too familiar way. Amber's critical gaze grouped the two together, matching Zachary's dark looks with this woman's lighter, but equally as dignified ones. No, perhaps dignified was only one aspect of it; there was a subtle command in the demeanor of both that instantly classified them survivors in life. Was Amber one? As the two doctors became involved in a more technical discussion—*why the need for that elbow link?* Amber cried silently—than she could or would follow, she strolled off to find out whether she could indeed resurface from each tiny devastation such as this seemingly innocent one. Heading for the most compelling doctor in the group—a poor second to Zachary, she was quick to acknowledge to herself—she devoted herself to conversation with him, keeping her back to Zachary and his lady doctor until the evening appeared at an end. Whether she had aroused any jealousy in him, though she certainly did not glue herself to this stranger as Zachary's friend had done to him, she would never know. For the chestnut-haired woman was still at his side, monopolizing him even as he bid good-bye to his colleagues.

With a pang of disgust, Amber prepared to leave. Then, she hesitated and, to her bemusement, proceeded to help herself to another cup of coffee and to settle into the large and comfortable sectional sofa in a most nonchalant way. It was as though some other being controlled her, willing her to fight for what she wanted. Did she want Zachary? One part of her, she knew, did very badly; all she had to do was to look at his lean muscular physique, clad this evening in an open-necked sports shirt and dark navy linen slacks, to relive her cravings. But did she want more? Could she accept the commitment that making love to Zachary would entail? For, in her mind, she could not give of herself without that commitment. Despite the image of the liberated woman, she was strangely traditional. There had to be love. Was there?

Her inner turmoil was belied by the outward calmness that possessed her as she sat, slowly sipping at the coffee, relaxing on the sofa as though it were her own. The lime-tinged eyes that slowly perused the room made it her own, studying every corner, every wall, every piece of furniture and decorative article, until she could close them and still see that which Zachary had built.

"Were you planning on sleeping here?" he asked in open amusement, his approach muffled by the thick shag carpet and startling her eyes wide open.

An instant flush spread from her neck to her cheeks. "I was just admiring your home—"

"With your eyes shut?" The dark brow that arched into his forehead dared her to speak truthfully, though the upward curve of his lips mocked her mercilessly. He stood before her, hands thrust in his pockets, the master at rest, so confident yet casual. The room was quiet; the others had apparently all left.

Amber felt impelled to speak truthfully. Her relationship with Zachary had been founded on the truth; they

126

had certainly shared enough of it to enable her the freedom now. "It's very comfortable here, Zachary," she began softly, drawing herself up straighter in the corner of the sofa to explain her feelings. "I couldn't help but"—her thick gold lashes flickered down, then rose again with determination—"close my eyes and enjoy the feeling."

His response was enigmatic, his blue gaze unfathomable in a way it had never been. Puzzled, she wondered if he understood what she had said. Impulsively, she stood, fearful suddenly of being forced by his presence to say things she might regret, things that might reveal the extent of his captivation of her. "Here, let me help you clean these things up." Her eye took in the assortment of cups, plates, napkins, and crumbs that littered the living room. Purposefully, she avoided the warm pull of his body, so straight and magnetic and masculine. For some reason, here in his home, her feelings were more exposed than usual. As she silently moved to escape him, collecting cups as she passed, she wondered just why she was suddenly affected this way. Had it been the meeting, seeing Zachary in action as a champion, the administrator of his cause? Without doubt, he had been magnificent at that. Had it been the presence of those two female colleagues of his, each attractive, as was her friend Corey, and each bringing out Amber's own insecurities? Had it been the subtle intimacy of one of those women, that one who had fit herself so closely by his side? Or was it merely her instinct to fight, a coming to a decision, that perhaps, since the first time since her divorce, there was, indeed, someone worth fighting for?

"You don't have to do that," Zachary ordered from the same stance with which he had watched her. "I can take care of it later." His voice sounded more tense; in the next moment, Amber knew why. For, from the bedroom area came the chestnut-haired doctor, seemingly disturbed about something though moving confidently to the sofa and sinking gracefully down into its folds.

The worst of imaginings coursed through Amber's suddenly frigid brain. A numbness seeped through her, as she woodenly put down the cups, rescued her purse and notebook from *that* woman's clutches, and headed for the door. Through it all, Zachary merely stood and watched her silently, his face a bronzed mask, even and unpenetrable. When she turned at the door, he was so very, very far away that a shaft of pain seared through that numbness. Her soft-murmured "thank you" was the only sound she was capable of, save a cry of anguish at the position she found herself in. *Damn it,* she loved him! There was no need to analyze the situation more deeply. She loved him! Without even intending to look, she had found a man with whom she was willing—no, wanted, even, needed—to spend the rest of her life. He was everything she could have asked in a man. And he was now back in his home, alone, with that attractive lady doctor—just as he had been on that patio with the raven-haired beauty at David's party the Saturday night before. Oh, yes, he was everything she could have asked in a man—with one gross exception. He had that same wandering eye which had crushed her once before in her life. She would not let it happen again. Why was it, her heart screamed, that men found loyalty so difficult to uphold? For her, it was instinctive; if Zachary offered her his love, he would have her fidelity forever. But he did not love her. And he felt no need for fidelity. Why, even at this moment, she mused, as she pulled into her own drive, he was probably—

That night Amber cried herself to sleep. Love should have been so beautiful. Why, oh why, she asked herself in agonized refrain, did it always hurt her so badly?

CHAPTER SEVEN

The following morning, Amber arrived at her desk to find a casually scrawled note across the top sheet of her desk pad. "Work Friday P.M.," it said. "We'll go to Haymarket afterward, then to festival at North End. Be in your office at 6—pick you up there. Z."

Dumbfounded, she stared at the note. It was the last thing she had expected to find when she arrived at work this morning, the last thing she needed to find after the tormented night she had spent, one that had left its mark on the pallor of her skin and the deep circles below her eyes. Two cups of coffee had done little to improve her humor at home; this note would do nothing to improve it now.

Confusion and anger created a whirlpool within her, churning furiously. After having been cordial but impersonal last night, then having flaunted his current bedmate before her nose, he had some audacity to leave such a note on her desk, filled as it was with the assumption that she was at his beck and call, on the job and off. Well, she fumed, Dr. Zachary Wilder would have another thing coming when he appeared at her office Friday to find that she had left at her usual one o'clock! There was no way she would willingly go out with him, particularly knowing as she did her one abysmal weakness, that of loving this divine but footloose man. The best course, she rued, would be one of a clean break; hopefully, she would be able to avoid him as much as possible, until the remaining four weeks of her job at this hospital were completed.

Mercifully, the time spent at the hospital for the rest of the week was in meetings with others of the staff, both PR and medical. Had she had the time alone at her desk, her mind might have wandered more. As it was, it took every bit of her mental strength to concentrate on the business at hand—that of drawing up the final blueprint for the major report on the proposed International Center for Sports Medicine.

Out of sheer annoyance at the presumption of his note, Amber made no move to inform Zachary that she would *not* be awaiting him at six o'clock on Friday evening. Guilt assailed her at her blatant breach of good manners. But the small voice within told her that he deserved to be stood up, that he would have to learn the proper way of asking a woman out, that he could just as easily go find himself a pretty intern—her stomach churned anew at the thought —to drag with him to the Haymarket. Not that she hadn't wanted to go to that particular area—for the Haymarket, the Faneuil Marketplace, the North End were favorite spots of hers. But with Zachary? Out of the question—or so she thought.

Six o'clock Friday evening saw her propped in a chair before the television set, catching the evening news with one ear while her hand, braced with a pen, began a letter to Scott. The child was thriving, as she had known, begrudgingly, he would. His letters and phone conversations bore out this fact. He needed a father—there was no doubt about that. Much as she tried to be the perfect combination, Scott needed a male figure to emulate, and would need one increasingly as the years of puberty approached. In momentary daydream, she wondered what Zachary would have been like as a father for her son. She hadn't seen him with his own daughter for more than a few minutes. Yet, even as she decried the inappropriate nature of the thought, she recalled the tenderness of his mien when he had turned to Liz on that first day Amber had ever seen him. The wealth of love in his expression when he had referred to Liz that day at the airport, then later in discussions they had had—all these things were proof of the type of father Zachary Wilder was. But, once again, Amber chided herself for the irrelevancy of the information. After all, Zachary surely did not love her and appeared to be in no rush, after his own unhappy marriage, to enter into that state again. Perhaps Liz managed very nicely between Zachary and the housekeeper, then her mother in the summers. What would it be like to have a daughter? Amber wondered. She had always hoped for more children, but it became a physical impossibility once Ron and she stopped sleeping together. What would it be like, she dreamed absently, to bear Zachary's child? The thrill of excitement brought her back to reality, a reality which seemed to exclude the possibility of that ever happening.

"Dear Scottie," she wrote, conjuring up the image of her son as he would read this letter. She missed him . . . and now she missed another. Why did love bear such pain?

When the doorbell rang, it was a welcome diversion from the rehashing of this last thought. Barefooted, dressed in shorts and a T-shirt, with her blond tresses barretted behind each ear to form two plaits of hair, she opened the door.

"Is your mother in, little girl?" His voice was velvet-smooth and melodious, filled with a humor that by rights should not have been there, considering he was supposed to have just been stood up. The gleam in his eye told of his following of her thoughts, yet it made no detour in its run of her body, taking in her outfit with an insolence that sparked Amber to life.

"Sorry," she barked curtly, "she's out." The door slammed shut again with a resonance that disturbed even Amber, who knew it was coming. Infuriated that he should show up here, in such good spirits no less, she stormed to the television, turned up the volume to drown out the knocking or ringing that she knew would follow, and crumpled back down in her chair, strangely drained. How could she survive if the mere sight of this man took so much out of her? He was so beautiful in such a very masculine way. Even with her quick glance just now, she had seen how spectacular he looked, wearing khaki-colored slacks, a raisin-hued shirt with a contrasting beige collar and the sleeves rolled up to the elbow, his vision fresh, clean, and manly . . .

Defeatedly, her head dropped onto her arms. What was she to do? How could she handle this type of persistence, this devastating charm? When she would have spit at him, he smiled, melting her resolve instantly. When she had wanted to see him, she didn't. Now, when she didn't, he insisted on showing up at her door. How had this summer become so very complicated?

The hand on her neck startled her. "Hey, relax! You're tense all over."

Green eyes uplifted to meet his blue ones. "How did you get in?"

His eyes flickered with a blend of amusement and accusation. "You left the back door unlocked."

So she had, she rued. But was she sorry? Really? The warmth of his hand had remained on the taut muscles of her neck, and she had to admit that his touch felt good, despite all the anger she felt toward him. How could one man have this kind of power over a woman? When the hand began to massage gently the muscles of her shoulders, she tried to pull away, but could not. "Just sit here and relax for a minute. Then you can go up and dress the part of the mature woman for an evening on the town."

The blond head which had fallen back onto her arms bobbed up once more. "But I'm not going anywhere—"

"Shhh, just relax."

The strength of his hands was potent medicine, sooth-

132

ing over all of the familiar lines and curves, conveying its order to relax and enjoy. Her back molded to his touch, its softness seeping beneath the skin and into her bloodstream, finding its way surely and inevitably to her brain, there producing a state of benumbed pleasure. He was like a drug, giving her a feeling of euphoria time and again. The expertise of his fingers kneaded her arms and shoulders and back to a state of delight, while she sat leaning over the arm of the chair with her head resting on her forearms.

He knew precisely what he was doing, touching her just to the point of distraction, then retreating. When she would have rolled over, he held her firm, his hands withdrawing in silent threat that she would only get as much as he chose to offer. And his renewed touch drove all possibility of anger at his domination from her mind. His hands were gentle, soothing, and understanding . . .

"So you really were going to stand me up?" he growled in her ear, his breath fanning her cheek.

"Yes." Her whisper was more from the dazed state he'd put her in than from any fear of his retaliation.

The pressure on her back increased. "And are you still?"

"Yes." Still a whisper, yet, to her ear, more of a whimper, filled with regret, but utterly necessary.

Abruptly, the soothing circular motion on her shoulders halted. "Why, Amber?" His palms felt her shrug an instant before he removed his hands completely and stepped back to the sofa, which would be out of her line of vision unless she chose to look at him. "Why?" he repeated, more harshly this time, demanding an answer.

The seconds ticked away on the watch by Amber's ear as she maintained her silence, slowly coming down from the state of relaxation to which he had brought her moments before. When the blond head finally shifted and her lime-eyed gaze slanted toward him, his rigid pose warned her that he would get his answer. "I'm sorry," she began with soft sarcasm, "but I don't make command performances."

His eyes narrowed. "What are you talking about—'command performances'?"

"Your note—you never once *asked* if I'd like to join you tonight."

Shifting impatiently in his chair, Zachary eyed her darkly. "Oh, come off it, Amber. Haven't we gotten beyond the formal invitation bit?" They certainly had in the physical sense, she knew, but there were other factors to be considered here. Fully recovered now from her temporary sensual flight, Amber sat up to face him.

"Perhaps you take too much for granted," she accused him, clutching her knees with either hand. When he said nothing, but continued to stare at her incredulously, she averted her own eyes awkwardly. The silence threatened to deafen her with its ponderous weight, yet she refused to break it. He would have to defend himself.

"Okay, let's have it," he spoke out, his voice steady, held in taut control. "What is it that's *really* bothering you? I know you well enough by now to know that you don't stand on ceremony. In fact, it's been just the opposite. Some of the best times we've had together have been totally spontaneous. Do you disagree?"

She could not, and shook her head reluctantly.

"Then, what's bugging you?" His head swiveled around toward the television, and he angrily reached over to slam the OFF button. "It doesn't look to me like you had anything better to do tonight. Why the put-down?"

There was so much she wanted to say, so much she would have blurted out had she not reminded herself of her own vulnerability. Instead, she faced him squarely, willing her voice to impassivity. "Why did you ask me to that meeting the other night?"

If surprised at her line of questioning, he revealed nothing. Leaning back in his chair as though prepared for a long, perchance boring interchange, his outward calm matched hers. They were two civilized adults, facing each other quietly, soberly, each with a bomb ready to explode inside.

"I thought you'd be interested in coming."

"Why?"

"The people were interesting, the subject matter relevant to your work."

"Was that the only reason you invited me?" Her courage came from some mysterious source within. She did not pause to question it.

"No. I wanted you to see my home." His gaze bore into her relentlessly, taunting her to look away. But she refused.

"I could have done that anytime. You could have simply brought me by there after a bike ride, if you had wanted," she reasoned, not quite sure herself of exactly where she was headed.

He nodded, lifting one hand to stroke the shadowed line of his jaw. "I could have, but this seemed more sensible."

"Sensible?" The line of her forehead creased in puzzlement. "Exactly what *did* you have in mind?"

The sudden exasperation which brought him to his feet took her by surprise, threatening her composure. "Look, Amber, what do you want me to say? I wanted you at that meeting. I wanted you in my home. I wanted to see you. Alone . . . more than anything. But it's very trying that way. Alone in a house with you, like this, I have one thing on my mind." His eyes shot toward the stairs in ample explanation of what that one thing was.

But Amber's thoughts were on that chestnut-haired lady doctor, the one to whom she had so docilely yielded at the conclusion of that evening. "Is that why you made sure your lady friends were at that meeting . . . and that one stayed long afterward?" she spat out, regretting her infantile tone instantly, but unable to take it back.

Tanned fingers cocked against the leanness of his hips, he stared at her for a long moment. Gradually, a knowing

135

smile slid across the length of his firm lips. "You were jealous!" he said triumphantly, drawing out each word for emphasis.

With a speed that had matched his moments earlier, Amber sprung up to face him. "I don't like being made a fool of, Zachary. And I felt like a grand one, intruding on your little after-business rendezvous. She is very attractive and must be stimulating in more ways than simply the medical. But how insensitive could you have been?" Her voice had risen in pitch until it was a near shriek, its venom directed at the gender of man, in general, and Zachary, in particular. He was no different from Ron, she concluded in torment.

"*You*, Amber, are *nobody's* fool." He was suddenly sober, all delight in her obvious jealousy having vanished. "If your feelings were hurt, then I do apologize. Beyond that," his gaze hardened imperceptibly, icy-blue orbs now chilling her in turn, "I owe you no explanations. As *you* once so aptly pointed out about yourself, I'm not used to answering to anyone, either. It's been a long time . . ." His mockery held an undercurrent of truth that stung her to the core. And it was to worsen. "Besides which, Amber," his teeth gritted against one another, "you have no right to act possessive—after your own behavior at David's party."

Suddenly, she understood. "So, *that* was it, tit for tat? Your lady doctor for my handsome photographer? He really got to you, didn't he?" Though she knew enough not to laugh at him, there was a strange satisfaction in the knowledge of his own jealousy.

When long fingers seized her shoulders fiercely, all satisfaction vanished, to be replaced by amazement. The force of his words and their strangled tone added to her bemusement. "My 'lady doctor' has a name—Ginny Warner. I'm sure I introduced you to her when you first arrived at the house; if you care to make accusations about her, do it by name. And yes, that young photographer did get to me.

You need someone mature, Amber, someone who has been through similar life experiences as yours." His eyes narrowed dangerously. "Does he know you are a divorcée?" His piercing, close scrutiny drew forth her head shake. "Does he know you have a nine-year-old son?" Again, she shook her head. "I didn't think so. Fellows like that usually stay away from women like you." He hesitated, analyzing her silence, coming to a tentative conclusion. "When are you going out with him?"

"Tomorrow night." She had almost forgotten about the date. In fact, there was little enthusiasm in its anticipation. Andrew Pasco was a poor substitute for Zachary Wilder.

The latter swore angrily, shaking her by the shoulders until her head reeled. "Damn it, Amber, when are you going to realize what is best for you? You have your life so beautifully in order except where it comes to men—and you're making a grand mess of that!"

Breathless and infuriated, Amber acted on impulse, a slender hand shooting up and across the dark-skinned cheek above her. "How dare you!" she screamed, frustrated and angry and acutely aware of the truth of his words.

"Yes, I *do* dare," he barked back, the livid red mark of her hand only slowly beginning to fade on his cheek, "because something tells me, deep inside, that you're worth it. I'll shake you and yell at you as much as I want, until I feel that you are beginning to act sensibly." His eyes blazed with a vehemence she had never seen before, yet she could only relate it to his desire for domination.

"You are an arrogant bastard!" she seethed, being held up now solely by his grip. "What makes you think you know what I want in life? How can you decide what is sensible and what is not? It doesn't seem to me that you've been any more successful with women than I've been with men!"

The last hurt him, denting his strength momentarily. When he came back, however, there was renewed fire in

137

his touch. "At least," his voice lowered to a determined drawl, "I intend to do something about that."

"Oh?" she fumed, a spitfire to the core. "And what might that be?"

His expression had softened subtly and the set of his mouth became less pinched. "I've been handling you all wrong, Amber. You need a strong man, one who can force you to make decisions, rather than one who gives you all the time in the world to make them. In the end"—his hands circled the ball of her shoulders to ease what he might have bruised in his anger moments before—"the decisions will be yours. But I won't wait forever." The further lowering of his voice to a husky timbre elaborated on his desire. "I want you and I intend to have you. Whether it is tonight, tomorrow, or next week is irrelevant. But I'm telling you now: I have no intention of leaving you alone."

Amber's throat tightened, choking off words for the moment. As always in this man's presence, she found herself floundering pathetically. His fierceness excited her as it angered her; his determination likewise. He *wanted* her—was that all, a physical need to be satisfied? And would she then be left, as she had been by Ron, when he chose to move on to more delectable pickings? Rebellion flared at the thought.

"You seem to assume that I 'want' you as desperately as you 'want' me," she began, her voice gaining strength with each word. "Well, you're wrong! I won't be manhandled and pushed around, just to suit your needs. And, I never said I wanted a man to begin with, let alone a strong or a weak one. I never asked for this," she cried, arguing to herself as much as to him. "I never wanted anything but a nice quiet summer filled with work and fresh air and relaxation. As for the last, it's been impossible, thanks to you!" Pausing to catch her breath, she also caught the smile that toyed with his lips, further irritating her. "And just what is so funny?"

He gazed down at her with a warmth that wiped out the anger his face had held moments earlier. "You look so . . . great, all hot and bothered like that . . ."

"I'm not hot and bothered!" A hapless bid to escape his grasp was thwarted by its tightening. His hands slid to her back to draw her even closer. "Let me go, Zachary," she warned, in a low and controlled voice.

"That's what you *least* want." The laughter in his azure orbs mocked her.

This time, she repeated her order more forcefully, accompanying it with a sharp but ineffective jab of her foot to his shin. "Let me go—I don't want you!"

"No?" His arched brow chided her dishonesty. But she had come too far to retreat willingly. She had to make a break. It would simply be impossible to live with his "wants" and her values, simultaneously.

"No!"

"I think it's time for your first lesson in reality, then . . ."

"Zacha—"

His name drowned in his mouth as it covered hers, his lips moist and compelling a response that she fought furiously. Wiggling madly to escape his embrace, she only managed to wedge herself more snugly against his manly lines as his arms tightened about her.

"No, Zachary, no . . ." she cried when he allowed her the chance to speak, then took advantage of her parted lips to plunder the recesses of her mouth with his tongue, drawing a deep shudder from her. As all shreds of reason fought his mastery, her body betrayed her. Her lips softened beneath his helplessly, then, slowly, slowly began the response he wanted.

"There," he crooned by her cheek, "that wasn't so bad, was it?" His mockery set fire to her again. Her palms shoved at his chest and she writhed to escape him.

"I won't give in to you, Zachary," she yelled frantically, fearful that her own awesome craving would make a lie of

139

her words. Her fear increased as his hands ran the length of her sides, his thumbs skimming the outer curve of her breast, then venturing inward to pinpoint their already taut bud.

"I'll give you a choice," he said, laughing softly and hoarsely in her ear. "We'll either go upstairs to bed right now, or you'll change into some . . . clothes . . . and come with me to the North End, as we had originally planned."

She gasped, part from the continued touch of his hands, part from the gist of his words. "*I* never planned any—"

"Then, it's to bed!" he exclaimed, swinging her off her feet before she knew what had hit her.

Desperate, she capitulated. "I'll go, I'll go!"

"To bed?" he drawled deeply by her ear as he raised a foot to the first step, then paused.

"To the North End."

Her feet slowly slid to the floor, though her body was still held to his by the arm curved about her waist. "Without any more fuss?" he asked softly.

"Yes." It seemed pointless to fight him; he would win anyway. Her eyes lowered to the button of his shirt for just a moment, before his thumb and forefinger cupped her chin and tilted her face back up. "Remember, Amber. No more Mister Nice Guy . . ."

She could have been a child, for the blatant humor that he directed at her. Yet, aroused as she had been by his body seconds before, there was no will to protest. "No more Mister Nice Guy," she heard herself repeat, a smile tugging helplessly at her lips. Strong hands turned her and, with a firm rap to her bottom, urged her up the stairs.

"You've got ten minutes. Pick something . . . feminine," he ordered, his blue-eyed gaze sizzling over her in anticipation. Without a word, she retreated to the privacy of her bedroom, remembering to close the door purposefully. Her quandary was the same, though somehow more distant now. A tingle of excitement surged through her as she lifted a bright yellow dress, scoopnecked and cap sleeved,

140

from its hanger. There was something very wicked about this new face of Zachary Wilder, and she felt in the mood for something wicked! He did please her—she loved him. Though she could never tell him that, his apparent determination to be with her gave her momentary pleasure. Because he had given her little choice, she had chosen the lesser of the evils, tossing her earlier resolve to the winds. She would take this evening moment by moment, savoring it, refusing to worry about what lay ahead. When the time came for Zachary to make good his threat of bedding her, she would fight him then . . . unless . . . unless . . . Could he possibly have the seeds of love within him, waiting to be released at her command? He spoke of physical desire, nothing more. Yet he could have easily taken her to bed right then; he had to know that, from the trembling of her body, so exposed by his caress. Perhaps he really *did* want her company, as well. Was that reason for hope?

Several moments in the bathroom was all she needed to freshen up. As the soft yellow fabric slid down over her shoulders to fall across her unencumbered breasts on down to her hips, she stepped into a pair of white high-heeled sandals, dabbed a refreshingly mild Yves Saint Laurent scent behind her ears, at the crook of her elbows, at the hollow of her throat, then lower, more daringly, to her cleavage, and sat down at her dressing table to apply light makeup to her face and secure her hair in a topknot far off her neck. That her smile seemed brighter, as a suddenly steady hand smoothed lipstick on her lips, was no mystery. This evening would be fun—she would make it so. Tomorrow could be damned, as could that Ginny Warner. But tonight, Zachary was all hers.

A strange shyness slowed her step as she descended the stairs. Zachary was at the bottom, the eye on his watch rising to catch sight of her. "Ten minutes on the dot. Good girl!" he complimented her. Where earlier she might have taken his humor as condescension, now she simply accepted it, word for word. His eye ran a thorough appraisal of her, however, and this she could not totally ignore.

"Do I please you?" The coyness in her voice was odd, foreign to her usual manner. But she did want to please him, very much. His gaze continued its study, flaming softly as she joined him at the foot of the stairs. Only then did his eyes meet hers.

"Very lovely," he murmured, then reached behind her to deftly pull the pins from her hair and let the blond tresses fall to her back. "*Very* lovely," he repeated with appropriate emphasis.

"It's going to be hot this way." Amber's warning was in reference to her hair, thick and luxuriant now over her shoulders as Zachary's fingers combed through it, spreading the strands in a sensual array of gold.

His voice was a deep groan. "What the hell, it's going to be hot, *anyway.* Let's get out of here, before I change my mind and opt for the bedroom." His lips feather-touched her ear as he ended with a whisper. Again, she was torn—knowing she should chide him for his one-track mind, yet thrilling at the promise of his ardor. Would she satisfy him? Could she satisfy him? Staunchly, she pushed that fear from mind, determined to make the most of the next few hours in Boston.

As always on a Friday night, the Haymarket throbbed with activity. Long rows of ancient wooden stands held the freshest of fruits and vegetables, all open, all ripe, all waiting to be tested, then bought, by the shoppers who ambled through. Signs of city turmoil were nonexistent here, for the narrow walkways were crammed with people such that a leisurely pace was enforced. Though Amber had lived in the Boston area long enough now, she was forced to admit in embarrassment that she had never been here.

"Never been to the Haymarket?" Zachary's disbelief was second only to the pride he took in initiating her to the rite. His long fingers wove between her more slender ones to lock securely as he led her past stall after stall of the open-air market. Sawdust was scattered underfoot, cushioning the wooden legs that held up the long, open trays. It was a gold mine for the artist, a still life in magnification. There were pyramids of bright yellow grapefruits and deep-toned oranges. There were mountains of lettuce, cabbage, and spinach, and forests of broccoli and carrots, plus a myriad of other fresh-grown offerings.

Each stall had its vendor, each vendor his unique personality. There was the quiet young man in faded denim overalls who carefully selected produce for each customer, the elderly veteran of the market whose haphazard costume reflected his style of tossing goods into bags, and the homespun woman whose sweet smile could sell even the most bruised of fruits.

Amber's eyes were as large and round as the greenest of the honeydew melons. "Fantastic!" she grinned, when Zach looked down at her for an instant before getting down to business.

He knew precisely what he wanted, pausing here and there to purchase a lemon, fresh peaches, tomatoes, and a head of lettuce, instinctively handing brown paper bags to Amber when his own arms grew laden. Reluctant to release her hand, he kept that close link between them, as their outer arms bore his purchases.

To Amber's amusement, when she began to wonder where she would put another bag, she found herself drawn down a stairway, one of many that forked off the main corridor of booths, and was led down into what she immediately discovered to be a butcher's shop.

"Dr. Wilder!" the proprietor, a small, wizened gentleman, buried in a once-white apron, now spattered with the proof of his profession, greeted them. "What can I get you this evening?" His accent was heavy, a Polish-American, Zachary whispered in her ear when the little man trundled off to the back room in search of the leg of lamb and the side of beef about which he had asked.

"You're buying a whole leg of lamb and a side of beef? Where do you put it?" she asked in amazement, her eyes falling to the slimness of his waist. "And don't tell me Liz will eat all that meat . . ."

He laughed softly, pausing to examine the samples the butcher had produced, then with a nod and his order, "The regular, Sam," he turned to Amber. "He gives me a supply which I can freeze. It's really much less expensive to buy this way, and the quality of the meat is excellent."

"But how will we cart all of this from here to the North End, then back to the car?" Their purchases now sat in a large pile on the counter. Her lime-filled gaze took them in dubiously.

Once more, her companion had the solution. "Sam will hold everything here for us until we return. Then, *you,* coach, will have to handle the bags while I—with my sturdy muscles"—his voice tickled her ear with its closeness and exaggerated note of seductivity—"haul the meat myself. Actually, it's not all that much. I only have so much money, you know." His eyes twinkled mockingly. "And if we still want to make it for dinner at Felicia's . . ."

Amber rose to the occasion, playing the part of the liberated woman to the hilt. "*I'll* pay for dinner," she declared, only to be interrupted sharply.

"You'll do no such thing!" The dark hair that fell across his forehead gave him a tyrannical air. That, combined with the vehemence of his tone, precluded any argument.

Amber's low whispered, "No offense intended," wafted into the close and suddenly pungent air, as she turned and walked slowly to the steps that led back up and out, waiting there for Zachary to join her. When he did so, his good humor was fully restored.

"Hungry?" he asked, his arm falling across her shoulder as they climbed the steps side by side. Amber could not

144

help but notice how well their steps matched and how delightfully protected she felt, held like this to his side. It was her own mind that put a dual meaning to his words; he had been totally innocent of it.

"Ummm," she conceded, not trusting herself to speak.

"That's good. Ever been to Felicia's?"

"Nope."

"Even better." As they talked, they made their way back down the line of produce stands, turned toward the North End, then crossed beneath the Expressway until they reached Hanover Street, the gateway to Boston's Italian district.

"By the time we're done eating, the festival will be in full swing," he explained, guiding her to the appropriate side street that housed the restaurant. "It's quite something to see—there are festivals throughout the summer. One is as exciting as the next. The flavor . . . well, you'll see for yourself later." He said no more as he ushered her into the restaurant. That he was enjoying himself immensely was obvious, and, in that, Amber derived much of her own pleasure.

What she ate or drank that evening, she barely noticed, other than being aware of the general excellence of the Italian cuisine, the cluttered gaiety of the atmosphere, and, above all, the potency of the man across the small table from her. He made the selections, ordering an antipasto and two main dishes—veal and fish—which they then proceeded to share. As the spicy aroma wafted about, they talked, warmly and freely, each of their own childhood, their upbringing, their family.

"Do you see your sisters and brother often?" she asked.

"It's difficult. They're as busy as I am. With Laura and Susan being doctors themselves, we meet at an occasional conference. Michael is freer occupationally, being an accountant, but his family ties him down." His eyes sparked in admiration. "He has four teen-agers and an eleven-year-old."

Amber spoke on impulse. "Would you have liked to have had more children?"

The deep blue of his eyes washed over her for long moments before he answered. "Yes. I still would. But . . ." He averted his gaze, denying her any hint of his thoughts at that moment. Fearful of pushing him lest his response distress her, she pursued a different course, only to find it, too, leading toward danger.

"Your parents must have enjoyed their grandchildren. Does Liz remember them?"

"They died when she was six. Yes, she remembers them vividly. She spent a lot of time with them while . . . Sheila and I . . . were having our . . . problems." His eyes held a faraway glaze as he continued to speak, strangely intent on sharing all of this with her. "My father died within three months of my mother's stroke. When she didn't make it, he more or less gave up. They had been like this." He raised his fore and middle fingers, straight and together. "They were both in their early seventies at the time—I was the baby of the family." His boyish smirk endeared him all the more to her. "I think my parents were badly affected by my divorce. Their marriage had been so strong; they assumed that any of their children's would be the same."

"Neither Laura nor Susan has married?"

"Susan did—briefly. There were no kids."

"Oh." Amber's fingers twisted around the stem of her wineglass. Anyone who coached a Little League team had to love children; her own experience had convinced her of that. Zachary must be a wonderful father, she mused wistfully. How nice it would be . . .

The deep velvet of his voice broke into her momentary daydream. "Come on, Amber. Let's go. The festival must be lively by now." Hand in hand, they wound their way between chattering crowds at the close-standing tables to the exit, where Zachary thanked the owner of the family-run establishment, paid the bill, then led her to the street.

146

The festival was, indeed, under way, with crowds milling down Hanover Street, through the heart of Little Italy. Cars had been banned from the thoroughfare, now, yielding to food and crafts stands and stands bearing religious ornaments directly pertaining to the celebration. For several minutes they stood in silence, watching the melange of activity before then. Amber breathed in the aroma of the street, a hearty blend of fried dough and peppers, spicy sausage, quahogs, and pizza. Her eye absorbed the colorful array of clothing, both on the patrons and on the stalls of clothes intermittently lining the sidewalks. Red, green, yellow, and blue were the colors of youth; the elders wore black, sedate and homely, yet they held as much appreciation of the holiday as the most jubilant of the youngsters.

Zachary held her close beside him as they slowly ventured down the street, pointing occasionally to a group of children on a high-slung balcony or an old woman leaning precariously from a window overhead, laughing with her at the sight of several young boys chasing their female counterparts through the crowds, squeezing her hand as they passed an infant, sleeping soundly in a pouch on its father's back while the melee continued all about it.

When he suddenly whipped her down a side street, she looked up at him, startled, to see an expression no less than triumphant on his handsome face, now darkened even more by the night shadows. "I wasn't sure which of these streets it was on," he explained lightly, pointing to an open doorway, through which another couple, much like them, had just emerged. "The best cannoli in the North End."

"But we've just eaten a huge—"

"This is dessert—for later, tomorrow, whenever. It's great. Wait and see." If she had any choice, she couldn't see it. Zachary called the shots. If he wanted cannoli, cannoli it was! Sighing with a strange delight, she followed him into the minuscule bakery. The small box with which they emerged several minutes later soon joined the others when they returned to the butcher's shop. As the BMW retraced the route from Boston through the western suburbs to Dover, Amber was to wonder about the abundant supply of food they carried. There was enough to feed them for a month, should they suddenly become stranded somewhere, far from civilization. What a lovely thought it was! To spend a month, alone and in solitude, with this incredibly desirable man . . . the thought sent twin spears of pain and pleasure through her. That would never happen, would it? It was the kind of irresponsible daydream which had led to her disastrous marriage years ago. Now, she was supposed to be older and wiser. And she had Scott, who would be returning from his father in less than a month. What would become of this relationship between Zachary and her, then? Liz would be returning also; how could he handle that?

"You're very quiet tonight. Did I really intimidate you?" he spoke softly, just loud enough to be heard over the purr of the car's engine.

Her blond head swiveled toward his, darker and now in profile as his eye held to the road. "Intimidate me? Impossible!" she lied, sounding unsure, even to herself.

A bronzed hand snaked out to snare her shoulder, its strong forearm curving beneath the weight of her hair and about her back, to draw her into the crook of his arm so that her head rested comfortably on his shoulder. Her body turned reflexively toward his, her hand fell to his thigh, causing him to curse softly under his breath.

"You'd better be careful, young lady," he whispered into the silken crown of her hair.

Burrowing more deeply against his warmth, relishing it to the fullest, she smiled. "You started it, Doctor. I'm merely giving you a dose of your own medicine—" Her voice broke off as he crushed her harshly against him.

"You, my little spitfire, may live to regret that witty tongue of yours. When we get home . . ." This time, it was his words that died, only the cause of death was not a

148

physical crushing, but a more psychological one. It was as though they were a couple, headed to the home they shared, after a happy evening out. Unsure as to whether he regretted having created the image, Amber savored it nonetheless. In his company, she felt at home, in every sense of the word. It was a heady feeling, full of speculation as to what the rest of the evening might hold.

Conversation was minimal as they transferred the meat, vegetables, and fruit to his kitchen from the car. Amber had not questioned their destination, intent on her wish to enjoy the evening minute by minute, following the dictates of the man she loved. When he led her back to the car and drove her home, she made no protest. When he deposited the box of cannoli in her refrigerator, then took her hand and headed for the stairs, she didn't resist. When he pulled her into the welcoming band of his arms, not far from the foot of her bed, she moved happily. Without thought of any other minute, there was no other place she would rather have been at this particular one.

As always, his lips lulled her as his hands caressed, coaxing the response which she so wanted to give. Driven to mindlessness by the fire of his touch, she found herself on her bed, its bedclothes pulled back and discarded as were hers. Yet Zachary remained dressed, resisting her attempts to caress him in return, to let her fingers find admittance to his chest, his arms, his body, much as his had already done.

His movement over her was sweet torment, a game where the players were his lips, his tongue, his fingers, and the board her body, pliant and aching for fulfillment. Soft words slipped helplessly through her lips, moans of pleasure, sighs of delight. When she begged for release, he held her off, retreating to an earlier stage of the game to build her to an even higher pitch. So sure was he of every step he took, that she didn't stop to question him . . . until she could take no more.

"Zachary, please," she moaned softly, groping in the

149

dark to find the touchpoints on his body that would arouse him to a similar state. His breathing was unsteady, proof of his own fired condition, yet he was in full control. The hands that had crept below the buckle of his belt were suddenly drawn back up to shoulder height by two larger ones which pinned them there firmly.

As he kissed her a final time, his lips held a clear smile. "Good night, Amber. Sleep well."

"Zachary?" But he was off the bed and gone, his footsteps echoing down the stairs, the door slamming shut behind him, his car leaving the drive before she could begin to understand what had happened.

CHAPTER EIGHT

Bright sunlight the next morning failed to enlighten her, either. She had been so sure that he would make love to her; everything in that evening had led up to it. Yet he had rejected her once again, this time seemingly as part of a preset plan, outlined in fine detail for his mind alone.

The night of sleeplessness had left her weary and drawn. Impulsively, she showered, threw on a pair of shorts, a halter top, and sneakers, hopped on her bicycle, and sped to his house. It could have been no more than ten in the morning, though she had absently left her watch lying on the bathroom shelf. Her bike stood by the garage as some uncanny instinct propelled her around the house, over the gentle flagstone walk to the point where the fringe of firs and head-high junipers gave way to a more open area.

His body caught her eye instantly, its gleam in the bright sunlight a homing signal. He stood tall beside a shallow hole, large metal shovel in hand, his head moving from the hole to a tree which stood beside it, roots balled neatly in burlap and wrapped in twine, topmost shoots no taller than Amber herself and a dogwood by species, if she guessed properly. Intent on his mental calculation as to how deep to plant the young tree, Zachary was unaware of her presence. She remained invisible, moving even further back to the cover of the greenery, as he bent to dig once more.

The rhythmic thud of the shovel as it pierced the earth steadied her breathing for the moment. She had come here in anger, she realized now, bent on determining his precise motivation for having treated her so cruelly last night, intent on venting her frustration on him. For, as surely as he had known she would go out with him that evening, he had known that he was *not* going to make love to her. It had been planned from the start; now, she wanted to know why.

But if she had come in anger, it vanished at the sight of him clad only in shorts and sneakers, his bronzed back glistening under a sheen of sweat in the hot sun. Muscles rippled with each thrust of the shovel, as the hole gradually deepened. His build was that of the athlete, a breathtaking body responding magnificently to the command of his brain. Rooted in her place of concealment, Amber's pale green eyes caressed the flow of that body, as she had been unable to do last night. Her fingertips ached to slide over the moistness of his skin, her lips tingled at the thought of mingling with his sweat, as every instinct of her traitorous body yearned to do.

As she watched the hole grow wider now, nearly ready for the planting, and the rugged and handsome body poised for a moment of rest on its rim, she could take no more. Turning, she fled, oblivious to the swivel of the dark head toward the rustle of the shrubbery and the subsequent shrug, as Zachary assumed that the squirrels were at play once more.

Her bicycle pedals rotated nonstop, propelling her toward home. Bursting into sobs on the pillow of her unmade bed, she surrendered to the torment of heartache, confusion, and unfulfillment that gnawed within. Where had that spunky young woman gone? she asked herself helplessly. Why hadn't she challenged him? Demanded of him? Forcefully sought the answers she needed so badly to know? What had become of the headstrong woman, who had built a life of security and stability for herself and her son? Reduced to tears this way, she failed to recognize herself. There seemed to be only one explanation. She was a woman in love, irrational and blinded to all too many things.

A cry of anguished determination brought her abruptly to a sitting position on the bed. Determinedly, she swiped at her tears with the backs of still-trembling hands. Zachary Wilder may have stolen her heart and taken with it a huge chunk of her pride, but she still had so much. There was Scott, her career, and, more immediately, a date with Andrew Pasco tonight. If nothing else, she would enjoy herself, *damn it!*

But determination was not enough. She was destined to failure. The whirlwind of activity with which she filled this Saturday, rather than giving her relief from her obsession with Zachary, merely exhausted her, such that, when the young photographer showed up at her front door at seven, she was fit company for no man. Makeup concealed the extent of her exhaustion, yet nothing could hide the lack of enthusiasm she felt in Andrew's presence. The drama production was inspiring, his conversation interesting, but terribly one-sided. After apologizing repeatedly to him for her unusual quiet, she was none too distressed when he suggested he take her home.

Puzzled by the difference in this woman, from the vivacious one he had met at the party the week before, he escorted her to her door in silence. "I'm sorry you weren't able to enjoy yourself more, Amber. Something is obviously on your mind." His sensitivity touched her, increasing her feeling of guilt. It would be unfair to see him again—if he bothered to ask. She had wronged him even this time, going through with the date when she knew that her mind was entirely preoccupied with another man. It was something that the other had said, which gave her the solution to her present quandary.

"No, *I'm* sorry, Andrew. It's been a bad spell for me. My son is away for the summer visiting his father. I've missed him." Gauging the surprised expression on her companion's face, she went on. "He will be back in several weeks. I don't think I'll be quite the same until then."

The photographer shook his head in symbolic dismissal. "Whew, I would have never dreamed you had a child. Well, good luck with him. Maybe I'll see you around . . ."

His back was turned quickly toward her, as he made his way to his car. Zachary had been right, she mused. Young and carefree men like this would run from thoughts of family and children. But not men like Zachary Wilder . . .

Where that thought left her, she didn't know. The next few days were miserable ones for her. She heard nothing from Zachary, nor did she catch sight of him at the hospital. Fortunately, the worst of the preparation for the final report was done; when Tony Leeter called her on her preoccupation, she pleaded exhaustion and left earlier for home that day.

The situation at home, however, was no better. Scott's letters came regularly, and she spoke with him every Sunday. Knowing that he was relatively content and well cared for, her thoughts turned to this other man in her life. Her gaze wandered to the telephone over and over again, yet it did not ring—at least, not at the instigation of Zachary Wilder. There were the usual calls from friends, all received with feigned good spirit—that vanished with the replacement of the receiver on its cradle.

The article on Little League had been submitted the week before. Diligently, she applied herself to one of several other intended articles—only to throw her pen down in disgust when her mind continued to wander to that dark face with the warm eyes which beckoned, beckoned irresistibly. How could she cope with him? She had met her match for wit and determination and sheer stubbornness. For there had to be a reason why Zachary hadn't called, why he had held his control in such preordained check

154

that last night they had been together. What was his plan? When *would* she hear from him?

If she had expected his eventual contact to be made with a victorious drawl to his voice, she was grossly mistaken. The fatigue which he was unable to hide when his voice filtered over the line to her on Friday morning startled her.

"Amber, it's me, Zachary," he began, when she had picked up the extension of the office phone in her own private cubby. "Look, I've only got a minute, but do you think you could get away for the weekend?"

This was not quite what she had expected when she had awaited a call all week. Determinedly, she held her frustration in check. "What do you mean—away for the weekend? That all depends on where—"

The deep growl that interrupted her was also uncharacteristic. "Don't argue, Amber. I'll be at your house at about four to pick you up."

"But, Zachary—"

"We have to talk. I've rented a place in Provincetown for the weekend. I'll see you later."

"I don't know—" Her words drifted off into a dead extension, moments after Zachary hung up.

If he had given her more time, she told herself, she would have made a personal protest. As it was, the morning was jammed with a department meeting from which she could not escape until one thirty, at which point there was barely time to try to track Zachary down in the hospital. Or so the rationalization went.

Four o'clock found her in her living room, an overnight bag on the floor by the door, her purse and car keys in her hand. There was still time to escape, she knew, toying with the idea of simply taking off in her own car and going somewhere other than Provincetown for the weekend. But the fact remained clear to her, as she slumped into the sofa, that she wanted to be with *him*. He wanted to talk. If it was a speech of farewell, he would hardly have suggested going away for the weekend. Instinct told her that

155

she would have to see this through. If the love she felt for Zachary meant anything, she had to respect his wish and trust his intent.

If she was paler and leaner for a week of distress, Zachary seemed no better when he appeared at her door shortly after four. Though groomed impeccably, he, too, seemed weary and less confident. Some strange will in Amber made her reach out to touch his hand when he stooped to lift her bag. Straightening, he gave her a smile of encouragement, then led the way to the car.

For three hours, they rode in near silence, exchanging only the most superficial of conversation. Yet there was nothing awkward in the silence. She felt the uncanny conviction that their minds were on the same wavelengths, that they were headed in the same direction. The car followed around the elbow of Cape Cod to its tip, where the colony of Provincetown lay, exposed to the whim of the Atlantic on all sides but one, that from which they now approached.

Parking the car before a stately old house, he slid from behind the steering wheel. "I'll be right back." His voice was soft and gentle. There was no harshness, but rather a strange element of defeat which Amber had not dreamed he could possess. Her eyes followed his lean form, outlined darkly in a navy jersey and snug jeans, as he mounted the steps of the house impatiently and entered. She clung to the sight of that front screen until he reemerged, a set of keys in his hand, to drive them further down the private lane until a small stone cottage came into sight. This time, when he parked in a rutted space, Amber jumped out, drawn irresistibly beyond the cottage to the ocean, which fronted it several hundred yards ahead.

The ocean—an endless entity, beckoning the heart to surrender to its depths in an emotional purge. The salt of the spray was a sample, a temptation. For Amber, this was her own release from all that was bottled within. The wind blew her silken hair away from her shoulders, gently buffeting her body as she plodded on, through sand soft and warm beneath her sandals.

As the waves clapped furiously against the shore in eternal rhythm, her thoughts were of love, that love she felt for Zachary. It had been there from the start, that something special which had passed between them this summer. And, endless as was the tide, so would be her love, regardless of what happened now.

The steadiness of the ocean's beat reverberated within her, giving her momentary strength. Turning, she looked back toward the cottage. There Zachary stood, tall, alone, and with an infinitely vulnerable cast to his eye as he studied her. Several steps brought her toward him, then she halted. More than anything, she wanted to ease his fatigue, relax his tension, erase the haunted look from his face. More than anything, she wanted to declare her love for him. Yet something held her back. Frightened and unsure, she held his gaze for long moments, the roar of the water behind camouflaging the rapid beat of her heart.

Then, slowly, Zachary moved forward, walking to within a foot of her. His eyes never left hers, probing the depth that held her love. But he was tormented. The war within him was obvious, tearing at him before her very gaze. The tapered fingers, that wanted to reach out to him, to help him, to comfort him, to touch him, were crammed harshly into the back pockets of her white pants. After his abandonment of her that other night, he would have to make the first move now. She just didn't know what it was he wanted . . .

As though hearing her thoughts, he spoke, finally, averting his eyes to the shoreline. "I had no right to bring you here, Amber," he began softly, taking several hesitant steps along the beach, continuing only when he saw her fall into pace alongside him. Puzzled, she merely waited for his explanation. His dark head was bent toward the sand, his hands, like hers, thrust in his pockets. Was he, too, afraid of what they might do if freed?

"I never wanted this to happen," he continued quietly, walking slowly and steadily, refusing to face her. "I've had one bad situation in my life . . . I had no intention of falling in love again."

Amber's pulse began to race despite the slowness of their steps along the beach. What was he saying? Did he feel . . . that . . . for her? Was it too much to ask in life that they might each find happiness with the other? Struggling to control the explosive state of her emotions, she bit at her lower lip, relaxing only when his voice came to her again, a near-whisper, barely audible above the sound of the surf.

"There was something different about you from the start. Just meeting you at that Little League game got me going. If we hadn't met at the airport, I'd have looked you up on my own. A beautiful hand with no wedding ring on it . . . was too much of a temptation." He paused, eyeing her tentatively, then turning more fully to face her when he saw her anguished gaze. "I've fought it as much as I can. I told myself to give you time, that you weren't ready, when it was *me* who wasn't ready. I resorted to macho tactics to convince myself that it was merely a physical attraction I felt. I've tormented you because of my own torment, and, in doing so, only made things worse." His eyes dropped momentarily in self-reproach, but lifted when he realized how much more there was left to say. "This past week has been hell for me, Amber. Forget the physical frustration—knowing you were out with that guy last Saturday night nearly drove me mad. I thought about you all week, wanting to call you, but afraid of what I would say and what you would do. I guess I brought you all the way out here so that I could . . . work on you." He shook his head in disgust. "Can you believe that?"

Knowing the force of her own love, Amber believed him completely. He had more courage than she had. Hadn't she turned and fled, that day in his garden, rather than to confront him as he was doing to her now? With his confes-

158

sions, Zachary had been man enough to bare himself before her. There was only one way she could handle that.

"I love you," she whispered, her words swirling around in the breeze to draw his head up with a start. When his eyes questioned her, she spoke again, louder this time and with the conviction she felt. "I love you."

Disbelief raged in the royal blueness of his eyes. His hands lifted to cup her face, tilting it up toward his. "Those are very strong words, honey. You'd better mean every one of them. I won't take them lightly."

"I mean it, Zachary," she beamed joyfully at him. "I do love you." In the instant, her breath caught as she was crushed against his chest, his arms falling to imprison her in their sinewed bands. When she raised her head to say it again, he kissed her firmly and possessively, decreeing by his lips that she would stand by her vow.

"Come on, let's go back to the house," he murmured against the softness of her lips, hugging her to his side as they returned to the cottage, leading her through the front room, where he had dropped their bags, into the bedroom where he promptly kissed her once more. "Last chance . . . are you sure?"

For the first time, she felt she could speak from her heart. "I've not been as sure of anything in a long, long time."

As though to make up for what he had done to her the weekend before, his own clothes were the first to fall to the floor, victim of his own hasty fingers. Amber saw him then, for the first time, beautiful and manly and highly aroused. When he approached her, she let her hands have their way, touching him with gentle exploration as he deftly removed her clothes, mirroring her actions when she stood as naked as he before the large double bed.

In one fiery moment of cataclysmic intensity, their bodies touched, his dark-haired chest against her soft breasts, his abdomen flat against hers, his ardency a source of hunger against her femininity. Preliminaries were unnecessary, having taken place in the days and weeks before. Amber's body thrilled to the violent passion that seized him as he eased her down onto the bed and made her his. She cried out in wonder at that moment of supreme union, aching with a fevered longing which was at last to be fulfilled. The sense of completeness that filled her as he led her to dizzying heights of rapture, enhanced the beauty of him in her love-dazed eyes. Her words of love echoed in his mouth as together they soared, higher and higher, exploding finally and simultaneously into a myriad of love sparks, falling at last in exhaustion from that height of passion to lie, damp and dreamy, in each other's arms. For Amber, it had been the ultimate declaration of her love, but one that bore repeating. As her hands played over the rugged lines of his body, she felt him stiffen and warm to her touch. Thrilled by her ability to bring him pleasure, she moved instinctively around and above him until he pulled her over his body to join them once more.

It was a lesson in giving for Amber, whose ecstasy derived from the delight she gave her lover, as much as from the strength of his body in her. When, a second time, they shimmered together, down from an apex of erotic luxury, she felt herself the woman, whole and new, rare and wanted, needed and loved. Arms and legs intertwined with his, she slept as he did, awakening only to satisfy the hunger that was insatiable, that seemed to grow greater with each satiation, that knew no bounds whatsoever.

Darkness fell in Provincetown, yet the low light that burned on the dresser was nothing compared with the flame that burst forth, again and again, throughout the night. Never had Amber experienced anything as spectacular as Zachary Wilder. All man, he was gentle and passionate, tender and electric, all-giving and demanding. His soft words of warmth and love in her ear almost made her forget that she had ever failed a man.

Dawn cast its blue shadow on her sleeping figure as he looked down, helpless to resist stroking the fine line of her cheek, chin, then lips. His "good morning, love" was whispered against her lids as she opened her eyes to see him. And it began all over again, the merest touch sparking a hunger that was mutual and sated only by complete possession, Zachary of Amber and she of him.

"We're spending the day in bed," he announced, when finally his breath steadied after the latest breaking of their passion's tide.

She looked up at him through the shade of tawny lashes. "Zachary, we can't do that!"

"And why not?"

"It would be . . . very . . . naughty." She grinned, triumphantly finding a word, any word to complete her thought.

Her slim body was hauled even closer to the long male one beside her, its textured surface tingling against her at every lengthy touchpoint. "That's right," he growled thickly. "For once in my life, I intend to be very . . . naughty, as you so delicately put it."

A soft giggle made its way through her passion-rouged lips. "You know," she whispered, "I feel like being naughty, too." Her fingers skimmed the surface of his chest, then fell to his waist before being captured in the first move of that eternally repeated game.

They did spend the day in bed, rising only for the bare necessities, snacking on the food that the proprietress of the main house was thoughtful enough to send—and diplomatic enough to leave on a tray outside the front door, with a strong-knuckled knock before she returned to her own house.

When not making love, they slept, ever in one another's arms, making up for the nights of the week past, in particular, when each had seen the dawn more than once. When neither making love nor sleeping, they talked, propped up in bed against one another, learning all those intimate details of the mind, as well as the body.

"Did I satisfy you?" she asked timidly, softly.

161

Royal blue eyes caressed her upturned face. "I've never been as satisfied by a woman."

"Have you been with many since the divorce?" There was so much she needed to know, so much she felt unsure of after her own crushing divorce.

He answered her reluctantly. "I've had my share. But none can compare to you, Amber. Please believe that." She wanted to, so very desperately, and she told him so.

"I think I'll always be unsure, after Ron. Perhaps you'll tire of me, as he did."

"Have I tired of you yet?"

"No."

"Well . . ." he crooned in proof.

"Zachary," she chided soundly, "it's been barely twenty-four hours!"

"And what a twenty-four hours it's been!" he exclaimed, with obvious relish. "You know that you belong to me now, don't you?"

Again she heard his own need for reassurance, understanding his insecurity as she did her own. "I've belonged to you since that day I saw you at the pond at Wellesley, standing so dark and mysterious by your bike. I can still picture the way you looked . . ."

Her sweet recollection was disturbed by his probe. "What about David's party . . . and that . . . what was he, a photographer?"

Amber laughed. "I was acting on the rebound at David's party. If you'd paid me any attention, I'd have looked at no one else. And as for Andrew, I'm afraid he's washed his hands of me."

"Are you sorry?"

Her blond hair tickled his throat as she shook her head. "I purposely told him about my son. You were right. It scared him off instantly!"

They both sobered at the subtle reference to Scott. It was a quiet reminder of the lives that lay ahead. It was not only a matter of Zachary and Amber in love; there were others to be considered. But this weekend was not the time for that, they joined each other in unspoken agreement. These two days were for the two of them, to live and love for the present, leaving the future to itself.

If the prescription was for carefree abandon, they followed it to the letter. Sunday found them on the beach, sunning, swimming, sharing the shore with each other and no one else. Amber glowed within, her happiness glittering forth in the sparkle of her lime-hued eyes which, more often than not, focused on Zachary. As they lay on the beach, stretched out beside one another after a vigorous bout with the waves, she let her head fall sideways to look at him. There was so much to him and their relationship, she mused, that she wondered if she would ever fully sort it out.

There had been, first and foremost, that chemical reaction, felt from their very earliest meeting. This weekend had been the culmination of that overpowering attraction; even now, her eye had only to touch the familiar lines of his face, his strong neck, his sturdy shoulders, to spark her instant response.

But there was more. As she had gotten to know him, she discovered a man whose depth of feeling, understanding, and compassion never ceased to amaze her. Even with their minor disagreements, he had known what she wanted. Perhaps even that dismal Friday night, a mere week ago yet seeming eons in the past, had been a lesson, teaching her how very much she did need him.

These two days of bliss had been as a dream in Amber's mind, a vision of happiness in her heart. Her love for him had deepened until she no longer knew where she ended and he began, so intricately intertwined were the two. From all outward signs, he adored her, reluctant to let her out of his sight—not that she fought him very hard on that score. His protectiveness made her feel warm and vulnerable and safe at once.

Even his quiet understanding of the slow silence that

seeped through the car on the return trip to Dover on Sunday night relieved her. Each passing mile brought them closer to reality, to the world of home, family, and career. For Amber, each passing mile brought with it a steadily growing fear that things would not be the same when they returned. Out on the tip of Cape Cod, in that charming cottage by the ocean, there had been isolation and insulation. Their love had blossomed there, unhindered, undiluted. Would the everyday world reveal thorns alongside that beautiful flower? There had been a headiness, a newness to their discovery of each other. Would this vanish with the lusty ocean air left behind? Neither of them was innocent in the ways of love, though there was a uniqueness to their joining that Amber, for one, could not deny. Would the harsher world of reality bring, even in her own love-shaded gaze, a flaw to their relationship?

The dark hand that reached to touch her every so often, to brush her lips or her cheek, to give momentary caress to her shoulder or a squeeze of encouragement to her thigh, could not fill the nascent hollow within. Throughout the weekend, there had been no word of marriage. What *was* their future to hold? Both Scott and Liz would be returning, each from his respective parent, within a few short weeks. Amber assumed that any talk of marriage would have to wait, dependent on the preliminary functioning of the foursome as a potential family unit. Suddenly, however, any wait seemed too long. There was a fiery possessiveness within her too which was unquenchable. Her fear was of losing Zachary, more than of anything else. That Scott would immediately take to the man had never been at issue; nor had the conviction that she could not have found a better stepfather for him. No, Amber felt a purely selfish fear take hold, one whose roots came from the hurt of her first marriage. For this one, wildly ecstatic weekend, Zachary had been hers. Would he be hers forever?

* * *

164

"Amber! Where in the devil have you been? I've been trying you all day!" The phone had rung within twenty minutes of her arrival in the lonely old house. "Scott was worried when you didn't call him this morning—he even called here, poor baby!"

"Calm down, Corey!" Amber urged her friend, pangs of guilt now joining with those other devastating fears. "I was away for the weekend. I spoke with Scott just a few minutes ago, when I first came in."

"Away for the weekend?" the other echoed, suddenly curious now that she knew her friend was safe and had been in touch with her son. "You didn't tell me about plans to go away?"

"It was . . . very . . . last minute."

Corey's broad smile shaped her voice. "Okay, so where did you go? Or"—her voice lowered dramatically—"is that classified information?"

Amber gently chided her for her dramatics, desperately hoping to minimize the impact of the weekend in the mind of this friend who saw through her so quickly. "It's no secret, Corey. I was in Provincetown."

"Alone?"

"No. Actually, I was with a . . . date." That certain something which kept her from blurting out the entire story to this, her best friend, mystified her. Yet she persisted in both her vagueness and her feigned nonchalance.

"A *date*? For the weekend? Who was he?" No waffling here, Amber mused wryly.

"Ah, Corey, you really don't want to hear all this. It was a weekend. I had a . . . great . . . time. Let's leave it at that."

"Who was he?" her friend repeated, bluntly ignoring the evasion. When Amber failed to answer, she prodded further. "Come on, love. We've shared too much for you to turn secretive all of a sudden. I'm your friend. Nothing you tell me goes beyond my lips!"

Corey was right; Amber had always been able to trust

her. Perhaps what was needed now *was* a sounding board, the latter reasoned, as she took a deep breath, then slowly exhaled it. "I spent the weekend with Zachary Wilder."

A pin drop could have easily been heard in the astonished silence that greeted her admission. "With *who?*" Corey demanded incredulously.

"You heard me. With Zachary."

"Oh, I heard you, love, but I can't believe it! You actually spent the weekend with *the* Dr. Zachary Wilder?"

Her friend's innocent exaggeration brought an involuntary grin to Amber's face. "Now what's so special about *the* Dr. Zachary Wilder?" she asked with her own innocence, *as if she didn't know.* "You were the one who was originally going to fix me up with him, weren't you? Or was it all a hoax?"

"Oh, it was no hoax, Amber. I had the feeling you two would hit it off. I just didn't quite expect . . . a weekend . . . wow!"

"Corey, you are impossible! We spent a weekend together in Provincetown. Just a weekend." Her inner fear made a foray to the outer world, causing her to bite her lip and hope that her friend did not catch the waver in her voice. Mercifully, she did not.

"*Just a weekend?* Amber, do you have any idea of what a weekend with that man is supposed to be?" A chill settled in Amber as she listened helplessly to her friend's chatter. "He is supposed to be *the* most delectable lover in the world! Rumor has it that *one night* with him is enough to spoil a woman forever. But a weekend? Boy, you got more than most. Was it worth it?"

Amber's heart caught in her throat at the implication of Corey's words. They had been offered in all innocence; her friend, happily married, would have no reason to make spiteful statements. But she had no idea of how Amber felt about the man, either.

"Amber?" The soft urging of Corey's voice reflected an awakening of sorts.

"Y-yes, it w-was worth it . . ." Amber's eyes filled suddenly with tears, which spilled helplessly over her cheeks. When her muffled sobs reached Corey's ear, the other was quick to respond.

"Oh, Amber, I had no idea. You're in love with him, aren't you?" Without awaiting confirmation, she went on, speaking as much to herself as to Amber. "I should have known, with your forced nonchalance, and all. You've been seeing him all summer, haven't you?"

Amber sniffled against the back of her hand, oddly relieved to finally be able to share this news with someone. "You m-might say that," she stammered, her breathing rough with lingering gasps.

"Should I come over now, love? We can talk—"

"No!" she began vehemently, then quieted instantly. "Thanks, Corey, but I really need to be alone, to sort things out. If I feel like talking, I'll give you a call."

"Does he love you, Amber?"

Memory of his words, repeated again and again, rang with symphonic splendor in her ear. "He says he does. But if what you say is true, if he moves around from one woman to another so quickly, maybe he was only infatuated, or—worse—lying."

"No, love." It was Corey's turn to scold her friend. "No other woman, that I've heard of, has had words of love. He's never made promises he didn't keep. And a man his age is not about to be infatuated, not with the situation he's been through during the last few years."

Despite the strength of her reasoning, Amber's distress raged unabated. "Well," she began, anxious to get off the phone and to the privacy of her thoughts, "he didn't make any promises to me, either. It may fizzle out as quickly as it began." Again, her attempt at nonchalance fell flat, the pain in her voice clear and sharp. But her friend took the hint.

"Look, love, you go rest. I'll be off duty until six tomorrow morning. If you want, give me a call. Okay?"

167

"Sure, Corey."

As Amber numbly hung up the phone, she thought of the only one whom she wanted to call. But he would be sleeping, or so he said. Visions of those last few minutes together flashed before her eyes, in vivid recreation of the scene.

When they had reached Dover, he drove directly to her house, carrying her bag to the door, his one free arm linked around her waist. He had kissed her then, reluctant to leave, his hands roaming her back a final time, then her face, his fingers caressing her features as though committing them to memory.

"Why don't you stay the night, Zachary?" Her spontaneous suggestion was on impulse from the heart.

A sad smile curved his lips, then tugged at her heart. "I'd like nothing better, honey, but it wouldn't be very wise. I've neglected the hospital, as it is, for the weekend. If I'm not in top shape tomorrow morning for rounds, they're apt to let me go."

"Fat chance," she chided him softly, her own arms locked behind his lean hips. "How *did* you get away for the whole weekend? I didn't even see that infernal buzzer anywhere." She had recalled, with a blush, its inopportune sounding on another occasion, and had not missed it in the least.

Zachary's grin held a bit of devilment in it. "I have friends in high places. I even managed to pawn the little box off on one of them. They had the phone number of the main house, in case of an emergency with Liz, but my patients just had to do without me for the weekend." The fact that the weekend had been hers so totally thrilled her, as did the words which next brushed by her ear. "Meet me at my office tomorrow morning at ten. We'll have coffee together. Sound all right?"

"Ummm," she murmured against his chest, the strong beat of his heart filling her other ear and her whole body with his life.

168

Now, alone and overcome by fears and insecurities, Amber felt that same pounding of a heartbeat in the blood that raced through her veins. *Good night, my love,* she repeated in silent litany. *Good night.*

CHAPTER NINE

The night dragged on endlessly, its emptiness a harsh reality after the days and nights of pleasure and haven in Zachary's arms. Come morning, Amber lingered in lengthy arbitration over her choice of clothes and her makeup, determined to make her most attractive appearance before him at ten. The vacillation of the night—he loves me, he loves me not—had yielded to an emotional limbo that cushioned her through her ablutions, dressing, and breakfast, then filtered around her as she drove to the hospital and put in a token hour of minimally concentrated labor on the last of the articles to be finished for the report on the proposed International Center.

Nine fifty saw her in the ladies' room, making last minute checks, recombing the hair which had been left loose at Zachary's preference. Nine fifty-five saw her waiting for the elevator, pulse racing impatiently in hopeful anticipation. Nine fifty-eight saw her tightly controlling her steps toward his office; nine fifty-nine saw her warm with excitement at the door that stood open, awaiting her arrival. But at ten o'clock on the button, her heart broke in two. There in Zachary's office stood the man himself, his arms about the shoulders of the same woman she had seen once before. The shapely legs beneath the dark skirt and white blazer would have given her away, had not her identity been revealed conclusively by the full chestnut mane that now cascaded over the same strong hands which had caressed Amber only the day before. It was Ginny Warner, his beautiful colleague, come to welcome him back to her arms.

For a long moment of disbelief, Amber stood frozen at the open door. Then, with a small cry of anguish, she turned and fled, blind to everything about her, deaf to the call of her name echoing in the corridor, as she found the nearest stairwell. She returned to her office, left word that she would be gone for the rest of the day, and escaped the suddenly smothering confines of the hospital.

The persistent ringing of her telephone held no interest for her. Even the possibility that it might be Scott failed to diminish her torment. But the house seemed to stifle her, much as had the hospital. Clear thought eluded her, as did that desperate breath of fresh air. Impulsively, she changed her clothes and climbed back into her car, driving aimlessly, stopping occasionally at a roadside spot to think, to mourn, to suffer anew.

She had seen it coming, one part of her declared. Ginny Warner had implied their intimacy that night at Zachary's house; it should have come as no surprise to find her exhibiting it this morning in his office. But after the past weekend, that other part of her argued—why had Zachary been partner in this deception? How could he have betrayed her so quickly, knowing all that she had once suffered in like manner?

She had been wrong about him, she knew now. His words of love had been shallow, motivated by a need he had felt at that particular moment. That the moment had extended over an entire weekend held no hope for the future. Corey had heard correctly. He was a superb lover, though he didn't stick around very long, once he had gotten what he sought. But Corey had said that he rarely spoke words of love . . . why had he to her, then turned to another as quickly?

Crying silently, she pulled to the side of the road once more. Where she was, she neither knew nor cared. There was nothing to return to, nothing to return for. The car found its way north, toward the communities of Marble-head, Gloucester, and Rockport, but the pain of the shore and its memories drove her further west. Hunger was nonexistent; when she needed gas, she stopped for that. In the end, she came full circle, returning to Dover in early evening simply because her muscles felt cramped and tired. Yet the ringing of the phone, audible even as she approached the front door, drove her away once more, this time toward her bicycle and the relaxation it always brought. Angrily she shunned the helmet which she had worn since *he* had first presented it to her; if he could be so duplistic regarding his emotions, she reasoned achingly, he was no more to be trusted regarding his own quirks. She had never worn a helmet before she had met him; she would not wear one now.

Anger drove her to reckless speed along the fast-dimming streets. Heedless of the encroaching dusk, she pedaled on, heading one way then the other, crying out when every spot turned out to be one they had passed together. Desperation bid her to take a wholly new turn, moving out onto roads headed east, further in toward the heart of the city. Perhaps the activity would divert her, she mused skeptically.

But she only grew hotter and more tired, finally stopping to rest at a landscaped rotary on the outskirts of Brookline. The automobile headlights failed to spotlight her as she sat, small and insignificant, on the soft grass, tugging absently at one dark strand after the other, remembering the healthy feel of *his* hair, as she had combed her fingers through it in bed late yesterday morning.

How had she let this happen to her a second time? she demanded in disgust. How could she have been such a fool? How could she have fallen for his line? She had been no more than a physical conquest to him; his words had merely paved the way for their lovemaking. Had he thought that she would not have given in to him without

172

those words of love? That she would have, only she knew! So taken had she been at the time, she would have given him anything he had asked, purely on the basis of her own love for him. That he had professed similar feeling for her and then had belied it so blatantly only made the loss a harder one to bear. In those two brief but divine days, she had held hope for a future filled with the richness of love, as she had always wanted it. Now, that future lay in a shattered heap on the floor of his office. He must have planned the whole scene, she gasped in sudden realization, as tears flowed freely from her eyes, blurring the car lights together into a glaring track of misery.

Mindlessly, she sat on that lonely spot of grass, the whir of the traffic moving steadily around her. If there was danger in her sitting, solitary and vulnerable, open to attack from the malcontents of the world, she couldn't have cared. In the maelstrom, only one idea held any meaning. She would go home. For the first time since she had left Maryland to attend college with Ron, she would return, alone, to her parents. If that was the only source of comfort, she would seek it out. The pain she felt at this latest catastrophe was too much for her to bear alone. Yes, she would return to Maryland until Scottie was due to fly home; only then would she come back here to make further decisions. The Public Relations department would simply have to understand that she had an urgent personal problem. She would have had only a few more weeks at the hospital, anyway.

These reasonings draining her, she mounted her bicycle and began the long ride back home. It was as though, having made the temporary decision to fly to Maryland in the morning, her mind was now a blank. Utter weakness spread through her, in repercussion of the horrible day that had been, as she forced herself onward, staying as close to the right side of the road as possible, adhering to all of the traffic rules and regulations. Pedaling further, yet seeming no closer to Dover, she wondered how and why she had come this far knowing that the return trip would be all the more tiring. Doggedly, she pushed on, shifting raggedly at the foot of each hill, inevitably climbing off before the top to walk the rest of the way, her thigh and calf muscles aching in rebellion, before the downhill gave her a moment's coasting respite.

Cars passed by occasionally, giving her leeway when the reflectors on her wheels caught the headlights. When one truck, a pickup, came frighteningly close and she swerved to miss it, nearly losing her balance on the shoulder of the road, she thought little of it. When a similar truck roared by a second time, closer now and accompanied by catcalls from decidedly male and perhaps drunken voices, she began to wonder. When it happened a third time, she knew herself to be the object of their game. The large side-view mirror barely grazed her elbow; trembling, she slowed, then stopped, following the taillights until they turned off onto another side street. Would the pickup come by for another swing? Should she take a different road, herself? Exhausted, she finally started off again on her course, fatigue preventing her from taking a detour that would add even the smallest amount of time to her destination. If she heard the truck come by again, she would simply stop and wait for it to pass.

Her ploy must have been anticipated, for this time, the pickup waited, patiently, behind the cover of another car, slowing as that car passed her, then gunning its own engine to terrify her. Panicked hands gripped the handlebars as she struggled to maintain her balance. The noise of the engine was on top of her before she could find a smooth place to pull over and stop. In a horrifying swat and a streak of pain, the side-view mirror hit her arm, forcing her to lose control of the bicycle, as she careened off the road toward a thicket of trees, where her front tire came to an abrupt stop, throwing her forward against a solid mass, then into a slump on the hard ground. There was pain and confusion, suddenly all physical, as some inner

174

sense told her she was badly hurt. Unable to move, the last thing of which she was aware was calling out for *him*. He was a doctor; surely he would help her. "Zachary! . . . Zachary! . . . Zachary! . . ." she screamed, until her voice trailed off into the silence of unconsciousness.

Her awakening was strange. It occurred slowly, mingling with a pain in her arm and her head. Unable to move, much less open her eyes, she could nonetheless hear the bustle of activity around her. Words and voices filtered through her daze, some more familiar than others, all with a note of concern that she felt had to relate to her. Every instinct within her struggled to make itself known, but much as she tried to speak, to reassure them that she was all right, no sound emerged. When the sounds about her grew quieter, she slept, hopeful that the morning would bring her the strength to rouse herself from this stupor. But whether it was morning or night, she didn't know. The voices swarmed around her again; still she could not respond. Puzzled by her apparent paralysis, she fell into a defensive sleep, unable to cope with her condition, any more than the doctors apparently could.

With each awakening came more familiar images, all from the past, most bringing pain. Her mind conjured up the pictures her eye could not, presenting before her a broken kaleidoscope of her life. She saw her parents and Ron and Scott; desperately, she cried out for him, yet no sound came. She saw her college days, the early days of her marriage, and felt the betrayal as the union fell apart. She saw her home in Dover, Scott at home plate, the first of her by-lines to appear in the local magazines. And she saw Zachary. It was his voice that called to her, over and over and over again.

"Amber, can you hear me?" it asked. "Amber, please try to speak. Do you hear what I'm saying? Amber?" Her brain issued the order to answer him, yet it went unheeded. One part of her cheered in triumph, sensing the pain

175

that her silence brought this man. It was just dessert, that small part reasoned. Why should she speak with him? He had betrayed her! Let him wallow in guilt . . .

But there were the memories of urges and feelings, desires and wants, all bidding her to reach out and touch him. His pain was her own; there was no escaping that fact. If only she controlled her body . . . but some other force did now. Try as she might, she could not break through the barrier of that semiconsciousness. When the frustration grew, she drifted to sleep again, awakening to a jolt of pain at the mercy of one probing hand or the other. Begging for relief, she remained silent, only able to listen and hear, a helpless spectator in an unknown arena.

Over a period of time, voices became familiar. There were doctors and nurses who stayed nearby, checking on her constantly, talking to her, expecting no answer yet always hoping. And there was the voice of Zachary, by her ear more often than any of the others throughout this ordeal. She listened closely to his conversation, trying to interpret the medical dialogue between him and his colleagues, unable to determine much beyond their own inability to do anything more. Zachary's words to her were saved for quieter times, when the drone of other voices had moved elsewhere.

"I'm right here, Amber. You're going to be fine," she heard him tell her. "If you can hear me, blink. Can you hear me?"

It was another lie, she decided, his assurance that she was going to be all right. Lies, all lies. She couldn't believe him. And she would certainly *not* give him the satisfaction of a blink! Stubbornly, she refused to acknowledge her hearing of him, though whether she would have been able to produce that one, simple wink, she did not know. She *did* know an emptiness when he finally left her bedside—an aching emptiness that had nothing to do with her physical injuries.

"It's all right, Mrs. MacLaine," one of the familiar

176

female voices came softly through to her. "Tears are a good sign. You keep crying and soon you'll be talking and laughing with us." A gentle hand soothed the tear from her cheek and her hair from her forehead, comforting her into a shallow sleep. When Amber awoke once more, the voices were more clear, the conversation more riveting. Every ounce of her strength was channeled, suddenly, toward the speakers.

"Any change, Zach?" It was a voice she knew she had heard before, a female voice, yet not instantly recognizable. The next was male and as familiar to her as her own, though tired and tense.

"Nothing yet. We just don't know . . ."

"It hasn't been that long—"

"Two days in a coma is enough! There's no physical reason why she isn't awake and active." His growing agitation was seized on by his companion.

"Take it easy, Zach. Your getting all upset won't help." Her voice was soft and steady, patient yet insistent. "She needs your reassurance. Chances are she may be able to hear you when you speak to her."

"I have. She makes no response. Nothing. The nurse thought she saw tears last night, but it may have only been a reflexive watering of the eye."

As a silence bit into the conversation, Amber realized where she had heard that other voice before. Zachary's next words confirmed that discovery. "This was all my fault, Ginny. I should have told her about our relationship. When she saw you in my arms the other day, she must have died inside. She's already been through something like this before. I should have told her . . ."

One part of Amber wanted to tune out again, the other demanded her continued presence. This wasn't at all what she wanted to hear. Better the meaningless words of encouragement from Zachary . . . than this sordid confession. Helplessly, however, she listened on.

"*I* was the one who asked you not to say anything to

177

anyone, Zach. You can blame me, not yourself. If I hadn't been as selfish, as demanding of your time, there never would have been the misunderstanding." Amber's senses grew more alert to catch the quieter response from Zachary as he evidently turned his head away from her to face Ginny Warner.

"You're my closest cousin, Ginny. I have always wanted to help you. It's been rough for you . . . trying for that appointment. You needed someone to talk to, and I was there. No, I should have been more insistent to Amber that she had no cause for jealousy. I should have told her we were related, even without revealing the extent of your professional dilemma." His voice returned to the bed. "I blew it. Let's face it—I blew it!"

In the silence that ensued, Amber struggled to comprehend what she had just heard. Had she been wrong all along, after all?

"You really do love her, don't you?" Ginny's voice came to her ears as it was directed toward Zachary.

His words were choked with defeat, low but clearly audible. "Very, very much. I wish you had gotten to know her, Ginny. She's warm and fun and loving . . . so loving . . ." His voice trailed off to join Amber's thoughts in instant replay of their weekend in Provincetown.

"I *will* get to know her, Zach," the soft voice insisted. "She'll come out of it, you'll see."

"Only if she wants to, and I'm not sure she does, after what happened on Monday. I don't know if you can understand, Ginny, but when I first met Amber, she was lovely and captivating and very obviously lonely. Oh, yes, her son had just flown off to California to be with his dad, just as Liz had left me. But it went beyond her son's absence to something deeper. I saw it because I felt it, myself. When there is that whole lot of love to give and no one to give it to, to share it with, there is a certain look of pain which one has. Call it indigestion of the emotions, if you will." He let out a harsh laugh at his semblance of

178

a joke, then sobered. "Amber had never been with another man, other than her husband. I wish I could have claimed that kind of morality." His voice lowered, as he went on more intimately. Amber wondered whether it was, indeed, her own pulse that had quickened, as she strained to hear every word.

"When we spent last weekend together, she was a whole person, Ginny. We were free and together. I'm sure she must have seen it in me—that same completeness, that same peace. She was beautiful and happy. She glowed, inside and out. God, how I love her." He paused. "She wanted me to spend the night with her on Sunday night. Maybe if I had, none of this would have happened. I shouldn't have let her out of my sight."

"That's unrealistic, Zach, and you know it," his cousin chided gently. "You'll be able to tell her everything . . . when she wakes up." It was left unsaid—that awesome *if* she wakes up—yet both quieted simultaneously. Finally, Ginny spoke again. "Her son—Scott. When is he due back?"

"In another ten days, I think. If she hasn't woken up by Sunday, I'll call him myself. She always spoke with him on Sundays."

"She'll wake up. She *has* to." Ginny spoke with such conviction that Amber almost believed her. "You just have to keep telling her how much you love her. You have to make her *want* to wake up."

I do! I do! Amber screamed silently, knowing now the full extent of pain which Zachary suffered. As she fought to free herself from her invisible prison, she heard Ginny whisper a soft good-bye to him. "I've got to run, Zach. I'll catch you later. Will you be back in your office?"

"No, you can find me here."

"Have you been making your rounds?"

"Phil has been covering for me."

"Been in the OR?"

"No."

"Zachary Wilder," his cousin rebuked him gently, "you know, you look like hell. If she wakes up and sees you, she's apt to go into permanent fright. If you can't work, just go and sleep for a while. How about it?"

"Later."

"Later . . . later . . ." she echoed his words, knowing that "later" would be only after Amber woke up. "If she only knew of your devotion . . ." she whispered beneath her breath, as her heels tapped soberly across the flooring, taking her to the door. "Call me if you need me, Zach?"

"Sure, Ginny," he murmured bleakly, his voice aimed still at the pale face on the pillow where his eyes held firm. For long moments, Amber felt herself suspended in a void between sleep and wakefulness. When Zachary spoke to her, she marshaled all her senses to respond.

"I love you, Amber. You have to know that. I'll love you forever. But I need you. Life would be so empty without you . . ." His voice cracked, mirroring her own break from limbo. The dark head dropped to her chest, his hands slid beneath the hospital garb to circle her back. In a totally unrecognizable sound, he wept, softly and soulfully, expressing the depth of his love as he could not have done in any more powerful way. Now Amber knew; if she could love Zachary forever, his love would be returned even more intensely. Slowly, and with the last bit of determination she possessed, she lifted her hand to stroke his head. His hair was thick and healthy, lusty between her fingers. As he cried silently, with the rich emotion of a man, she repeated her motion, soothing him with every bit of her caring. She loved him so very much, this wonderful man who had come into her life such a short time ago . . .

With gaining strength, she lowered her head to kiss his. Instinctively, his arms tightened their hold, crushing her to him, heedless of the physical injuries that had brought her to the hospital in the first place. Amber cried out, slowly, impulsively. "Aaaah . . . Zachary . . . be careful . . . that . . . hurts!"

Though her voice was a weak-whispered croak, he heard it. His body froze for an instant before he slowly raised his eyes to hers, terrified that he would find it had been a product of his imagination, this voice he had heard. It held her spirit—but had his own need conjured it?

The warm green pools of her eyes were open and brimming. The face that had been still and pale now took on a hint of pink and a thread of animation. Slowly, her lips softened into a deepening smile, cutting through the tears that dampened her cheeks.

"Amber . . ." He spoke her name in a long drawn-out whisper, its sound a caress on his tongue. "You've come back . . ." His gaze was blue as the ocean, buoying her even as it drew her into its depths.

Her nod was faint but distinct, her lips moving soundlessly. "I love you." The words were shaped and conveyed. Then, in reward for the effort it had taken to pull herself from her trance, she witnessed the slow drain of tension from his cherished features. When he smiled at her, the reflexive flip-flop within her told, beyond a doubt, of her recovery. Straightening, he lifted her to him, cradling her body now as a fragile treasure. The hospital mattress yielded beneath his weight as he sat on the bed, holding her gently, tenderly, refusing to set her back from him for even the shortest moment. When his face lowered and his cheek brushed hers, the salt of their tears mixed, then gradually dried, one and the same, it no longer mattered.

"Zachary . . ." That her voice sounded weak and distant was minor; that it had emerged in response to her brain's impulse was the triumph.

"Don't talk, honey. You've been through so much. Please rest for me." His soft croon was a potent relaxant, as was the beat of his heart by her ear. A lingering tremor

181

of anguish passed from his body through hers, to disappear forever.

"I'm sorry, Zachary . . ." she began again, driven to tell him all she'd learned.

"Shhh. We'll talk later."

"No," she whimpered softly. "I was wrong . . . very wrong. I had . . . no idea . . . about . . . Ginny." She paused, breathless at the mild exertion. But the same determination that had brought her from her coma now pushed her on. "I love you . . . and thought . . . it had happened . . . again. Do you . . . understand?"

His gentle rocking motion lulled her, his hand smoothed silken strands back from her face. He held her cheek against his chest, needing time to compose himself. He wanted to be strong for her—strong to love and protect her, strong to provide a haven for her always.

"I know, honey. We've both been through that." His pause brought with it the full implication of her words. "You *did* hear me talking with Ginny!"

His hand felt the nod of her head, his body the deep breath she took. "I was hurt and angry . . . and tired that night. I'm still . . . not quite sure . . . exactly what . . . happened."

Sufficiently composed now, he laid her gently back upon the pillows. He needed to look at her, to see her, to convince himself that she had, indeed, returned to him. Lifting her hand in both of his, he nibbled at her fingertips, not once taking his eyes from hers. Her recovery was a miracle for which he would spend the rest of his life giving thanks.

"What *did* happen, Zachary?" she whispered, aware that only one of her hands was free to cling to his.

The sigh of relief he offered told her immediately that whatever the damage, it was minor compared with the coma she'd been in. "You must have been the object of a stupid game of chicken. The driver in front of the pickup

182

was worried and went back to check, once the truck whizzed by."

"But what happened to *me?*"

"Oh, nothing much," he grimaced, wrinkling up his nose for emphasis. "You broke your right arm when you fell—sorry, no writing for a while," he teased sternly. "And you took a bad bang on the head. That accounted for the unconsciousness. But, beyond that, you're bruised . . . that's all."

It was a strange feeling, to know so little about one's own body. Skeptically, she eyed him. "Are you . . . sure? You're not keeping something from me, are you?" she asked fearfully.

His smile exuded confidence and reassurance in its breadth. "Now that you're out of that coma, everything is going to be fine. Just fine." Gentle fingers traced the sculpted line of her cheek, as his eyes caressed her again.

Her doubts vanished instantly, as did her smile, as the clearing of one muddled issue led to the urgency of another. "Ginny was . . . right, Zachary! You do look . . . terrible! If I hadn't heard her warning, I might have—"

His mouth covered hers to smother any further sound save that of her soft moan as she surrendered her heart and soul, fully and finally, to him. His lips were sweet and gentle, rich with promise of good things to come.

"That's one sure way to shut you up," he said smirking down at her, at last, drinking in the look of utter happiness on her face.

"Ummm," she murmured, suddenly tired but satisfied, her eyes closed and savoring her mind's image of him, her hand gripping his with a strength that astonished him.

It was the moment he wanted, before she drifted off to sleep. "Say you'll marry me, Amber." Falling somewhere between question and command, the force of his intent sent an explosion of joy through her weakened body.

Tilting her head sideways toward his face, her eyes were heavy-lidded and dreamlike, her smile spreading in he-

183

ralded acceptance. "I will marry you," she whispered, knowing intuitively that her future would be nothing without him. "You won't leave me, will you? Ever?" Half-asleep, she struggled to hear his answer, her hand tightening convulsively as she waited.

Unashamed, he let his tears flow once more, as he lifted her hand to his lips. "Never, Amber. Never." The knot in his throat precluded all other talk, but none was needed. He had made the promise she wanted to hear. And Zachary Wilder, she knew, never made promises he didn't keep!

CHAPTER TEN

"Shall I carry you over the threshhold?" The rich resonance of his voice sent a thrill of excitement through her, as the arm that encircled her shoulder drew her to a halt before the door of his home.

"But Zachary, we're not married yet!" she protested with mock coyness, struggling to keep her delight in tow.

"Bah! That's just a formality—more for the benefit of Scott and Liz than anything else. You're my wife *now*, Amber, for better or for worse."

Her left arm tightened around his waist. "Ah," she crooned, "that sounds so nice." With a backward tilt of her golden mane, she offered her lips for his kiss and was not disappointed. His lips met hers with a flame of passion that branded her his as no marriage license could. His hands were less steady when he finally released her and fumbled for the key to the front door, opening it at last, then pausing. From the threshhold to Amber and back, his eyes spoke of his mind's calculation. Then, with a devilish gleam suffusing his features, he swept her off her feet and into his arms, carrying her from the heat of the day into the coolness of his home, his body providing the only warmth she needed. Gently and with exaggerated care, he lowered her into a corner of the sofa, propping the pillows behind her, fussing to make sure she was comfortable before standing back, legs planted apart, hands on hips, to survey his work.

"That should do! Do you feel all right?" His overwhelming concern, considering he was a doctor himself and had to know how far along the road to full recovery she truly was, pleased her.

"I'm fine!" The clarity of her lime-shaded eyes reinforced her declaration.

"No pain?"

"No!"

"Any headaches?"

"No!"

Satisfied, he turned to leave. An instant frown creased her features. "You're not just going to make me sit here idly like this, are you?"

His broad grin chided her for her nonsense. "Of course not! What you need is a tall, cool drink, then some lunch." He rubbed his hands together, delighted with his role of nurse for a change. "First, the drink." With the enthusiasm of a small boy, he bounded toward the kitchen.

Amber's eyes followed him until his broad back disappeared from view. He most certainly was not a small boy, she mused, but rather the very mature and loving man to whom she had committed herself for life. The thought thrilled her again. He was right—she was his wife already, though the actual ceremony would wait another two weeks until the children were both home. The children! And he wanted more, he had already informed her. Once she had dreamed it; now, her dream would become reality.

Looking back, the past three days had been part of that dream. From the moment of her awakening, she had been treated like a princess, pampered by all of the hospital staff and, in particular, by Zachary. Her doctors—Zachary had been denied that privilege, being so emotionally involved with her—would have discharged her a day earlier, had it not been for Zachary's insistence that she remain in their care until he had rearranged his schedule sufficiently to allow him to take care of her at home.

"But I don't *need* constant care. I'm fine! This cast is not all *that* inhibiting," she had half-protested at the time,

186

despite her craving that he be with her every minute.

"I want to be there," he had insisted, putting all doubts to rest. "I won't have it any other way." There was no resisting his determination and stubbornness; and Amber would have it no other way.

So she gladly acquiesced, resting that extra day, though grateful when the PR department sent a secretary up to take dictation of her parting thoughts. Her strength returned with each passing hour, as Zachary saw to his affairs, ably distributing his caseload of patients among his colleagues to allow himself time off.

"We'll be going to London next month for a conference on the International Center," he informed her, to her surprise and delight, during one all too brief stop in. "The children won't have begun school yet; why don't we take them with us?"

Amber's eyes lit up. "That would be terrific! They'd love it, and so would I. But . . . won't we be in the way?"

His mock-frown stilled her worry. "My family . . . in the way? Of course not! While I'm at meetings, you and the kids can be exploring. During the evening, we can do things together."

Sudden shyness brought a blush of impatience to her cheeks, painting them a healthy rose. "Will we . . . have some . . . time . . . to ourselves . . . ?"

No less eager than she to claim his marital rights, his mind had moved along similar lines. "I've got two weeks of vacation coming," he announced with a sly grin. "I'll take them now, before the kids return. We'll have a honeymoon *before* the wedding, if that's all right with you." His slow drawl at the last dared her to disagree. As he sat on the edge of her bed, his long arms straddling her hips, his face was deliciously close and delightfully wicked.

"It's very naughty . . . but I love it," she had giggled mischievously at the time. Now, as she caught sight of his tall form returning to the living room, a large glass of lemonade in each hand, she giggled again.

187

A dark eyebrow arched in speculation. "And what is *that* about?" He stood lean and well-muscled before her, as attractive as he was charming, dressed for relaxation in a sport shirt and jeans.

Her eye darted from his as she blushed. "I was just thinking of our honeymoon. We're really doing it differently, aren't we?"

Suddenly serious, he knelt down before her, cupping her chin with his bronzed fingers, turning her gaze back to his. "Everything about this love is different, Amber. Everything about this marriage will be different, too. You'll see." His thumb feather-touched her lips, parting them gently, then receiving her kiss before she spoke.

"I know it will, Zachary. I love you so much . . ." The ache of longing in her eyes was matched by his, both undeniable. Her hospitalization had imposed the kind of abstinence which, given their soulful declarations of love to one another, was painfully trying.

"Here, drink your lemonade." His voice came through thickly with its needed intrusion, the hand which thrust its tall glass into hers a reluctant diversion. He had vowed that she would rest, for the next few days at least. The question remained as to whether, given the explosive chemistry between them, he could live by his vow.

His eyes, pouring into her helplessly, told their story. Aware of his restraint, Amber made a mirroring gesture. "I enjoyed meeting Ginny. Once we were properly introduced"—she emphasized the words in teasing accusation —"we got along beautifully. Is her chance for that appointment as dead as she seems to feel?" Ginny, herself, had told Amber of the possibility of her appointment as chief of anesthesiology at a large medical center in North Carolina. It was an appointment she had wanted badly, but one that had been touch and go for weeks. Now it looked as though she was to be rejected primarily because of her age.

"There's still a chance, as long as the final decision

188

hasn't been made," he explained. "But it doesn't look very good. It's a shame—she's good. If only she were five years older, with five years' more experience under her belt . . ."

"That's a funny twist. Usually women wish they were younger." Her casual observation brought his royal blue eyes back to spear her.

"Do you?"

"No," she answered instantly, softly. "If I were five years younger, I would not have met you. And, even if I had, I would not have had the maturity to be the kind of woman you need. There are moments when I still worry." The old fear came back to haunt her, clouding her eyes momentarily. "I've failed once—"

"You'll *never* fail me, honey," he began vehemently, then his tone quickly altered, "unless you dare to go biking again without a helmet. You deserve a sound spanking for that!" He recalled vividly those few nightmarish days when she had been unconscious, when he had wondered whether she would ever rise to recognize him again. His eyes glittered dangerously, sensuality mingling with legitimate anger. "At least you had the good sense to keep screaming my name. That motorist caught it before you passed out. If the police hadn't brought you directly to the General, I might not have found you for days. Do you believe *now* in wearing helmets?"

Suitably chastised by his gruff tone, she lifted rounded green eyes with appropriate timidity. "Yes."

"And will you promise to wear one whenever you ride, from now on?"

"Yes."

"And will you insist that the children wear them when they ride?"

"Yes."

"Good!" Frowning sternly, he looked away from her to take a long drink of his lemonade. Amber followed the movement of his hand, his lips, then his throat as the cool liquid drained from the glass. The throb of the pulse at his neck mesmerized her, taking a toll on her resolve.

"Zachary . . . ?" Her voice was a mere whisper, innocent though with a definite sensual lilt.

"What?" he barked.

"Kiss me . . . ?" Among the many secrets they had shared in the last few days, she had learned the sure-fire way to humor him. Now she resorted to it with unabashed pleasure.

"What—" His dark head swiveled toward her golden one.

"A kiss," she moaned, feigning pain. "I need . . . a kiss . . . right . . . now . . ."

His anger fled as quickly as it had sparked to life. Yet he clung to his sobriety for all he was worth. "You *need* a kiss . . . ?"

"Badly," she begged, her eyes widening in silent pleading. It was simply too hard to be near him; there was an element of truth to her words, despite their more impish origin.

The sternness of his expression melted against his very wish. An involuntary force drew him down onto the sofa beside her. "Amber," he warned, calling on his last bit of sanity, "you need rest." The inches he put between them had already begun to diminish.

"*Bed* rest," she taunted him softly, grinning pertly as she shrugged away all propriety, all inhibition, all reserve.

His lips twitched at the corners as he struggled to withstand her devastating allure. At last he shook his head, surrendering to that spirit he admired in her, that spirit that had captivated him so long ago at the baseball game. "What am I going to do with you, Amber?"

She had the answer instantly. "You can begin by making love to me." She rolled her eyes skyward, as though to enumerate all of the little erotic things that that might entail. "And while you're at it, you could—"

"Amber, you're shameless! I'm never sure what you'll

190

come up with next." Her graphic demonstration was more than he could bear. With a deep groan, he swooped down to seize her lips beneath his own in a kiss born of intense need, crying of urgent hunger. "You are enchanting," he murmured, deep and low, against the softness of her cheek, then abruptly halted his wandering fingers. "You won't knock me with that thing, will you?" His head cocked to eye narrowly the large white cast which rested up against the back of the sofa in readied pose.

Amber laughed gaily, feeling free and frivolous. "Now why would I do a thing like that?"

His blue-eyed gaze took on a deeply sensual glow, sending sparks of desire through her. His voice held the huskiness that spoke of his need. "Because," he began, lifting her into his arms easily and striding from the room, "I'm going to take you to my bed and make very passionate love to you. Right now."

Her unencumbered arm coiled possessively around his neck, her fingertips reveling in the thick hair that tapered to his nape. "Thank God!" she whispered against the strong column of his throat, "I thought you'd never get around to it, what with lemonade, then lunch, then—" Her teasing ceased abruptly as her back hit the bed and her eyes caught the love in those above her. Gasping, she remained still, mesmerized by the intensity of feeling held therein. The time of play, of light banter, of gentle conversation was in the past and the future. In the present there was only love, yearning for expression in the most exquisite form of communication two people can know.

Reaching up, she drew him to her, offering her lips, her body, her essence. She loved him to distraction, as he loved her. Never again would they be apart. As their bodies became one, this knowledge was shared, bringing each a joy never known before. It was ecstatic, it was electric, it was endless—this love. And it was theirs.

LOOK FOR NEXT MONTH'S
CANDLELIGHT ECSTASY ROMANCES™